# Hideout Hotel

# HIDEOUT HOTEL

### Janine Alyson Young

STORIES

CAITLIN PRESS

Caitlin Press Inc.
8100 Alderwood Road,
Halfmoon Bay, BC V0N 1Y1
www.caitlin-press.com

Text and cover design by Vici Johnstone.
Cover image iStock 000019292484

Printed in Canada

Caitlin Press Inc. acknowledges financial support from the Government of
Canada through the Canada Book Fund and the Canada Council for the Arts,
and from the Province of British Columbia through the British Columbia
Arts Council and the Book Publisher's Tax Credit.

Library and Archives Canada Cataloguing in Publication

Young, Janine Alyson, 1985-, author
        Hideout hotel / Janine Alyson Young.
Short stories.

ISBN 978-1-927575-46-8 (pbk.)
        I. Title.

PS8647.O6247H53 2014        C813'.6        C2013-908507-6

*for Alex*

# CONTENTS

# BUSHFIRE

I PUKE OUT the bedroom window because Mum is in the kitchen making coffee and I don't want to see her. My sister Marley pulls the sheet over her head, judging me, but she used to drink even more than me before she got knocked up.

I'm still in my clothes from last night and my shirt is sweaty. I lean out the window and spit on the red dirt, then fall back into bed. My neck is sore. I turn my head from side to side and wonder if there's any damage. The lampshade beside my bed is crooked. I reach up and adjust it.

Marley flips onto her stomach. She drapes an arm over the side of the bed. She shifts and the mess of her hair appears beneath the sheet, then part of her face.

"You shouldn't lie like that," I tell her. "You'll squish the baby."

"What do you know?" she says.

I tell her it's common sense. She's five months along. She's not really showing, but she's fatter and her tits are huge. She always grabs them and complains that they hurt. For once I reckon I'm the better-looking one even though I'm shorter and my face is rounder. We've got the same beer-coloured hair and tiny teeth, but everyone could always tell us apart.

She yanks the sheet off and looks around. It's not even ten but it's already too hot. I reckon it'll be fifty today. Outside two kooka-burras fight. Their wings beat the dust as they lunge at each other.

"Why's it so messy?" she asks.

The dresser drawers are open, clothes strewn everywhere.

"Rough night," I say. I wish I'd cleaned up before Joel drove her back on his way to the mine this morning.

I had a run-in with our old man last night when I came home. He was drunk and wanted to set me straight from something he figured was his business. I don't want to think about it, and I definitely don't want to talk about it, especially with Marley.

We lie for a while and listen to Mum's spoon on the counter, then packing tape on boxes. Today is moving day. We're not moving; our parents are. They're going to Kalgoorlie. Mum transferred to the hospital there, and Dad took early retirement from the mine. I reckon they're going because they can't stand us anymore, or because Dad can't stay sober here, but they just say they need a change.

They announced their move on the morning of our eighteenth birthday a few months ago. Marley found out she was pregnant around then. I can't remember if she'd already told them, but they must've talked about going for a while so I guess it's safe to say they weren't leaving because of that.

The morning of our birthday our old man lumbered out of his bedroom, poured himself some coffee and sat down at the table with us. It was strange to see him up at that hour, his hair stiff, in shorts instead of work clothes. He worked the graveyard shift at the mine and always slept until two in the afternoon.

I'd avoided him pretty well until then. He was always after me about something. Not so much Marley, even though she was the one running around with Joel getting pregnant and whatnot, and I worked full-time at the sheep station and drank nights, just what he'd always done.

Our mum stood there in the doorway of the kitchen with a plate of sausages and told us they were leaving. Our old man shifted in his chair, pulled papers out of his pocket and laid them on the table. They'd gone to the bank in Esperance and signed the trailer over to us.

We could keep it or sell it; it wasn't worth much, but it was something to help us out.

"It wasn't my idea," he said. He thought it was a no-good place for girls. "You two'll get the worst of it if you don't smarten up."

I couldn't understand that, keeping us here all our lives if he didn't think it was right, then criticizing us when we wanted to stay. It's our home. It isn't that bad. Sure it's a shithole, but every place is a shithole in some way.

Marley turns over and asks what time I work. I tell her I don't. She wants me to take her shift. She's still a comber. I've been moved up to shearer but I still work for her sometimes when she's too tired or if I have nothing better to do. I cover for a lot of people. It's better to keep busy, but I have two days off and I won't give them up.

"I just worked nine in a row," I say. "And I covered you on Monday."

My big plan for the day is to sit at the Pony Hotel bar and drink until I can't remember my name. A wave of contractors finish a stint at the mine around seven tonight and they'll stay in the Pony's motel before going home, or wherever, until the next contract. They usually live out in the mine's bunks because there's not enough room at the Pony for everyone, but sometimes they come in to party. It's good to have goals and tonight I have two: get drunk, and get laid.

"She's packing the pots!" says Marley. It definitely sounds like the pots are getting packed. Mum wasn't sure if she'd take them or not. She said she'd order us some new ones but they won't arrive for three weeks and Marley suddenly likes to cook. "I'm supposed to make a family supper before they leave."

"I'm not coming," I say quickly. I reckon Marley's scared about being on our own with a baby on the way. She's got Joel but he's not much of a provider. Lately she's been pushing the family time, trying to get everyone together. But Mum's been busy packing, Dad seems to hate me, and I don't want to see either of them if I don't have to.

"Gina," she whines.

"I've got plans."

"What? Getting drunk? How is that a plan?"

"Because I'm *planning* to do it," I say.

"You can go to the bar after," she insists. "They said they're leaving at nine."

My parents travel at night because my old man drives and he hasn't slept a night through in twenty-five years. I sigh and stare at the ceiling. There's a line of ants above the dresser. They weren't there yesterday. This sort of thing is our problem now. I grab a shoe and bang the wall. Fire ants. My stomach stirs so I nudge the window open. There can't be much left to throw up; I forgot to eat lunch and I definitely didn't have supper.

Marley is up. She grabs clothes from the floor and stuffs her drawer back into the dresser. She's pissed off, and probably trying not to cry. I could tell her I'll come to dinner but I'd be lying. I want to dissolve into the bed. I can't stand it when she's mad at me.

"Marley," I say. She bundles up her work clothes and slams the door.

When I hear the shower start I grope under the bed for the bag of peas I used as ice last night. The carpet is damp and the peas are soft. I stand at the window and toss them far, between the eucalyptus and the dirt path.

I have some time to kill before the bar opens but I head over to the Pony anyway. A couple of men mill around the front doors smoking, not looking at each other. No one likes company in the morning, especially drunks. Once they get inside they can disappear into the dim bar, forget it's daytime altogether. I'm looking forward to that myself, though I can't shake the feeling of disappointing Marley and last night and my parents leaving for good. I'm still queasy and I need a beer before I'm going to feel better.

I don't like to wait outside with the drunks so I walk under the balcony by the front doors and call for Casey. Her room is the farthest one to the right. Her doors open and she pokes her head over the railing and waves.

"Catch you at a bad time?" I ask. She's wrapped in a bedsheet.

She makes a face and shakes her head. She's going with Jesse but he's away for the month. She wouldn't touch another guy, not because she's against that but just because she thinks all the men here are dirty. She's from somewhere near Adelaide. She started as a barmaid a few months ago and was desperate enough to stay for the money. She doesn't realize all men are the same; Jesse's no different from the old miners, just younger.

She disappears, and a few minutes later she's clothed and un-locking the front door.

"Not open yet, mates," she says to the men crowding in, nearly kicks them back. "Ten more minutes and Tam'll be down."

I slip inside and follow Casey blindly to the kitchen as my eyes adjust. She goes in and comes back out with a cold steak sandwich.

"We have a new cook," she says. "He's such a pig."

"What happened to that kid with the broken nose?" I like being in with the Pony gossip now that Casey's around.

"He showed up for his prep shift railed," she says. "Bill figured he couldn't keep his shit together. God, he'd only been here a week."

I follow her into her room. There's a double bed, a wardrobe and a warped mirror. The double doors open to the balcony and we go out and sit at the table. Sometimes I come up here after the bar closes if Casey thinks the guys I've met are too sleazy. She walks me home after everyone disperses or gets someone else to.

No one lives up here except for the staff and by staff I mean Casey and Tam, and I guess this new cook. The head cook lives in the basement; he has his own room down there and wants nothing to do with anything after he's done at the grill. Sometimes incense and pot waft up the stairwell.

Casey passes me half the sandwich, then gets up for her cigarettes and a pack of cards. She comes back with a couple of glasses, too. I don't smoke, but she nudges the glass toward me.

"What is it?" I ask.

"It's *water*, Gina. Jesus."

I make a face. "That's disgusting," I say, wiping my mouth.

Casey snorts. "How do you survive?"

"Pop, beer, juice." But I chug the rest because I'm actually thirsty. It's too hot out, even in the shade of the verandah.

The view is nice up here. You can see almost everything: the General Store, the gas station, the coffee shop, and the off-sale liquor store. There's my old school, the one-storey brick building, kindergarten to year twelve. Behind that is the community pool where the senior kids are splashing around. I bet my friend Val is down there. She was a year behind me. I think it's only her and her cousin in year twelve this year. Everyone else dropped out. I don't know how she can stand it.

I glance out over the red dirt and scraggly bush. There's a bushfire somewhere in the hills near Jerramungup and when the wind catches it you can smell it. Not a good sign for the sheep stations. They've been trying to get it under control for weeks now but it's been crawling east.

The only thing you can't see is the library that's also the police station; that's behind the Pony as you're coming into town. But everything else is along the highway. At the edge of town the highway forks—you can either follow it west, which leads back to Perth, or go straight into the desert. A few days later you end up in Adelaide. I haven't been too far in that direction, or the other for that matter. I squint to see if my parents are outside loading the moving truck. Our trailer is off the dirt road on the left with the others.

"Are you coming to our party tomorrow?" I ask.

"Sure," says Casey. She deals our cards but they blow away.

She gets up and chases them down the verandah. "What's the occasion?"

"My parents are moving."

"Where?"

"Kalgoorlie." I tell her how they left us the trailer. I want to tell her how Marley is mad at me, and how I probably won't say goodbye to my parents before they leave, but I don't. "We can have parties all the time now."

Casey frowns. "So are you going to stay here?"

"I guess," I say. I haven't thought about doing anything else. Tina's leaving the station in May, and I reckon I'll be promoted to floor manager. I'd hate to see the job go to anyone else; I'm the only reliable one.

"You should come travelling with me," says Casey. "I'm leaving in a couple of months."

"My sister's baby is due in June."

"Oh, right." Casey concentrates on shuffling the cards, then takes a drag of her cigarette.

"You shouldn't smoke," I say, watching her. "It's bad for you."

She flicks the butt over the railing and keeps shuffling the cards. Finally I grab them and deal, even though I don't know what game we're playing.

We go downstairs and Casey disappears behind the bar to help Tam change a keg. Some girls I grew up with sit around a table by the door and as I climb onto a stool and attempt to ignore them, Brittany calls me over. A fortress of strollers and babies surrounds them.

"Where's your sister?" Fran asks.

"Work," I say. They all frown. How can she still be shearing at five months? What's wrong with Joel, making her work?

"Maybe if she had a *sitting* job," Amber says.

"She actually just sorts. It's not that bad," I say, but what do I know? She hardly does anything anymore but Randle can't fire her.

"Still." Amber shakes a bottle for the baby on her lap. "All I could do was lie in bed and eat when I was pregnant."

Two of their little boys whack each other with pool cues. Casey eyes them as she dries the glasses. The girls chain-smoke and toss their butts on the floor. I've never actually seen an ashtray in here. Burns cover the linoleum and every once in a while the maintenance guy comes by to sweep.

Fran buys me a double and the girls complain about their kids and boyfriends. I don't like rum and Coke. It's too sweet and it makes me puke sooner. I just want my beer. It's after noon and I don't even have a buzz on yet. I glance at Casey and make a face while the girls discuss what a loser Joel is.

Joel lives in a hitch trailer at his dad's across from the Pony. He and his brothers grow pot in there and he talks about how once the buds mature he'll have it made. Marley sleeps there a lot but she won't move in. He promised her they'd have their own place before the baby is born, and conveniently now they do, except that I'll be there, too.

I guess there are worse guys to be knocked up by. He's trying at least. But when they first got together, just before she got pregnant, we had a party while our parents were away. Joel was there with Marley but he came into the toilet while I redid my hair and closed the door.

"You're beautiful," he said and grabbed my belt loop.

I told him he just thought that because I was Marley's *twin* and to get a life. I stomped on his foot and beat it out the door. Marley was in the living room holding a beer as the guys explained how a water bong works, but her eyes searched for Joel. I grabbed my shoes and a couple of cans and ended up wandering around town. I think I slept on a lounge chair at the pool that night and when I came home the next morning I pretended I'd gone home with someone. He never tried it again so I didn't say anything, but I always make sure I'm never alone with him.

Marley has a pile of bridal magazines beside her bed. They'll get married sometime after the kid is born because Marley thinks pregnant weddings are tacky. She shows me her favourite dresses and asks what I think. How the hell should I know? I don't think I've worn a dress once.

Most of the girls we grew up with have kids and boyfriends they think are deadbeats. If I had to put my money on any of them, I'd choose their men. The guys might be bad, but at least they don't pretend otherwise.

"What about you, Gina?" asks Brittany. I look up and they're all staring at me. Brittany taps her long fingernails on the table. She wants to be an aesthetician but you have to go to Esperance for that and she hasn't saved any money to move yet.

"Sorry, what?" I take a gulp from my glass.

"Are you going with anyone?"

Amber says, "Yeah right," and gets up to stop the boys from climbing on the pool table.

Fran coughs. "Don't you know Gina likes them older?"

Then she leans in and asks if it's true I slept with Amber's dad.

"What? No." At least I don't think I did. Admittedly, there have been a few rough nights in the last couple of months.

Casey collects our empty glasses and asks if we want another round.

"Not everyone can spend the day at the bar," says Brittany as she gives Casey the once-over. She stoops to lift a baby from the floor. As she buckles the stroller she asks when Marley's baby shower is.

"Isn't it a bit soon for that kind of thing?" I mean, I don't know much but I'm pretty sure you have those right before the kid pops out.

"You mean you and your mum haven't planned anything yet?" She sighs.

I remind her that our mum is leaving.

"Oh, right." She waves one of the boys over. "That's so *sad.*

How can your own mother leave when you're about to give birth?"

As they fumble through the doors with all their babies and strollers I hear them make plans for the shower. I grab my phone to see if Marley's called, which she hasn't. I sit at the table and hold the warm rum and Coke. Through the window I watch the girls shuffle down the sidewalk, grab at the boys dodging in the street, flap their hands as they yammer at each other. I look down at the drink, pick the straw out of the glass and chug the rest.

At four every afternoon the day-shifters quit the mine and if the men don't pass out at home they sit at the bar. Sometimes they sit together but usually they scatter out and watch the TV. They lay their money out in front of them. Casey rings their drinks in, helps herself to the pile, returns their change and just has to keep their glasses full.

I put my cash out, too, and stare at the screen. The horses pound the track on mute. Once in a while someone gets up and places a bet at the machine by the pool table. Tam comes down and takes over for Casey. She gets a break for a couple of hours until the night shift.

Dave, the owner, comes in at one point and changes the channel to the news. The reporter stands behind a billow of smoke and explains the bushfires are under control in Jerramungup but they are spreading to the grazing country. No one pays much attention except for the guys signed up for volunteer fire control. They raise their heads and finish their beer and eventually take off to sleep; they might get called out later.

I've had a few now, but mostly I'm just tired. I pick up my phone. It's almost six. Marley finishes work soon. I wonder if the family meal is on and if anyone will bother to call. Before the supper rush the day-shifters leave. One of their kids comes in and says either Mum's in the car or can they have some money because there's no food in the house. Or no one comes for them, and they get up one by one and lumber out on their own.

The Pony had a real reputation before the new owners bought it a couple of years ago. It used to be called the Hideout. No one calls it that anymore except a couple of stubborn old-timers. It was dimmer and dirtier. My old man used to take me there sometimes after I turned fourteen. They didn't mind if you sat and had a couple beers if someone was responsible for you. He never took Marley, though. Once in a while they even hired skimpies to come in and serve.

Then Dave and his wife bought it, opened the drapes and stopped catering so much to the contract miners. They gave everyone three warnings to smarten up before they were banned. It was never clear if our old man was kicked out or not, but eventually he stopped going. For a while the barmaids just refused to serve him Jim Beam because that's what always did him in. I'm not sure if it was out of spite, that he couldn't stand being denied, or if things got out of control one night. Whatever happened he never comes to the Pony. It's the only place in town I know I won't run into him.

Some of the banned men moved, couldn't handle not having a place to let loose at the end of the day. I reckon the town changed because of that. A few new families moved in, and the worst of the contractors took jobs up in Kalgoorlie instead. The most entertainment we get now is a guy who does Neil Young covers once a month. Tam's off the hook for some reason, maybe because she's permanent, but Casey has to wear a low-cut Emu Export shirt. Some of the men still treat her like she's a skimpy when they've had too much, but it's not like it used to be.

The contractors will be in soon. Dave lugs kegs up the stairs. I get up and go to the toilet. I lean over the counter and examine my teeth, then take my hair down. I've got nice hair; it's long. When I turn around in the mirror I realize my crack's hanging out a little and hitch my jeans up.

At my place at the bar, where I left my phone and beer, I find Marley. Her eyes are puffy. We go and sit at a window seat in the dining room because she doesn't like the smoke. She used to smoke, and I still catch her once in a while, but she's trying hard to stop. Tam comes by and Marley orders pasta for both of us, even though I don't want anything. I roll my eyes. She's become more and more maternal.

I ask her what's going on.

"They just left," she says. "They were all packed up when I got home from work."

"What about supper?"

She shrugs and wipes her nose. "Mum was upset. She was in the toilet crying when I got in and Dad just wanted to go."

I swallow. I wonder if they asked about me but Marley doesn't say anything. They're actually gone, just like that. No apologies, no goodbyes. Kalgoorlie is only a six-hour drive, but we won't be going anytime soon and our parents never mentioned visiting.

"What a prick," I say finally.

Marley's always been the favourite. No one ever hit her or gave her much of a hard time. She didn't take sides when I complained about them. She doesn't realize how fucked up we all are. If I told her about what a hypocrite our old man is—coming home drunk last night, lunging at me while our mum just stood in the hallway—she might get it, but I don't see the point now.

"Forget about them," I say.

Marley looks like she'll cry pregnant-style. I brace myself and catch Tam's eyes as she approaches with our supper. I shake my head and she turns around and heads back to the bar with the plates. I reach across the table and dig my nails into Marley's arms.

"We've got our own place now. We can do whatever we want."

"I just want my baby to have a family."

"What do you mean!" I say. "It's got you and Joel and *me*. I'm not going anywhere, ever, not without you and the baby."

I get up, push her down the booth and get in next to her. I grab her and imprison her in a hug. She gets snot on my shirt so I let go to give her a napkin. Her boobs overflow the top and sides of an old tank top, stretch-marked.

"Your boobs are huge," I tell her. I say that almost every day. Mine seem to be smaller, if that's possible. She smirks, then frowns and clutches them.

"They hurt," she says, and squeezes.

I find our dinner at the bar. Marley eats but I just pick at mine. Eventually Joel comes in with some of his buddies.

"Bushfire's getting closer," he says. "You can smell it in the air."

"What are you doing here?" I ask, narrowing my eyes.

Marley jabs me under the table.

"I'm hungry," he says and grabs a menu. "What, I need your permission?"

I make a face, but slide my supper over to him.

By the time Marley and Joel leave, the place is almost full. It's rare to see a full house: we hardly have the population for that. But almost everyone is here, plus all the contractors. I recognize some of them, but most aren't familiar. Some are still caked in gold dust from the mine, clean goggle circles around their eyes. But most have cleaned up, trimmed their nails, put on some real shoes and shaved. They've been underground for weeks; to them this is like being back in a city. The place smells like aftershave, nicotine and whiskey that's been on the breath for years. I go over to the bar. I'm ready to get shittered.

At the jukebox I pick out some AC/DC and join Mitch McBride for a game of pool. He's a few years older than me and our mums worked together at the hospital. He's probably the only guy in the place I wouldn't sleep with, not because he's not good-looking but just because he's kind of like a brother. Besides, he's not interested.

"You on the prowl, Gina?" he asks, catching me stare at a group of miners as they shout for another round.

"Maybe," I say. "Which one should I go for?"

"If you want to know what I think," he says, waving to Casey for another beer, "I think you should take your time. You're practically the only girl in the place."

I look around. It's true: there aren't too many other women around. We play a game of pool and I lose, as usual. Mitch goes out for a smoke and I decide it's time to mingle. I sit at the bar for a couple minutes before a small dusty guy comes over and buys me a drink. He doesn't talk much, just sips his beer and eyes me.

Eventually I get up and talk to a couple of miners. I let them put their hands on me. I don't care. No one needs to let loose like these guys, and they buy me beers. There's no one I'm especially interested in, but I'll settle once it gets late enough.

Tam's behind the bar pouring pint after pint, and Casey's in the corner taking some guys' orders. She doesn't look like she's having fun, but I'd love to have her job tonight. I walk over.

"You ever been a skimpy?" I hear one of them ask her. "You sure got the, ah, skill for it."

"Just tell me what you want, mate, or I'm walking away."

They all laugh and one of them shouts, "Jugs!"

She rolls her eyes at me but I just grin. She heads off to the next group but one of them follows her. He's got short shorts on, and big dusty boots and a long jacket. He looks familiar but I can't place him. He doesn't look like he's here to party. He's up to something. I watch him follow Casey for a while; then he leans in to say something to her. She skitters away behind the bar with her head down and passes Tam the orders.

Later, when I come out of the toilet, she passes me and slams through the kitchen. The door swings back and forth as she shouts something. Poor Casey, she's really letting it get to her tonight. In the hallway back to the bar I see Boots-and-Shorts linger by the stairwell. He looks at me and spits on the floor, then turns back to watch the kitchen.

❖

It's around ten when I see him coming through the door: Rudy King. He's probably forty, tanned and thick-skinned with blond hair and a gap between his front teeth. He's big, manly; I've been watching him for a long time. I used to think he was a pilot, but that was a joke he told the barmaids. He's just a miner. He's been taking contracts here for years and comes into the Pony every few months.

I go over and stand by him for a while until he turns to me and nods. He buys me a beer and I sit with him and his friend. They don't talk to me much, but eventually Rudy glances at me and asks if I'll come upstairs with him. He doesn't have to ask twice.

I follow him up. The floorboards creak down the hallway. His room is number fifteen, the one beside Casey's. The motel must be full, otherwise they wouldn't book anyone up here. The bed is a single. It seems out of place with its yellow sheets and flowery blanket. There's a packed duffle bag on the floor and a pair of boots by the balcony doors. I start to pull my pants down and Rudy tells me to turn the light off.

The hall lights and streetlamp off the balcony come in through the panes above the doors, and music and random pounding from downstairs vibrate the room. It's like someone could burst in at any moment. I fumble for a lock but can't find one.

A take-away bag rustles and Rudy slumps on the bed and cracks a beer. I take one, too, and sit next to him. When he's finished he tosses his can on the carpet and grabs me. I try to put my beer down upright because I'm not done yet. He peels his shirt off. He smells like chew and something spicy. I lean down to kiss him but he pushes me back and we get going. I go slow for a while; I want to enjoy it. But soon he flips me down onto the bed and lies on top of me. I wasn't hoping for romance or anything but it's nice to be comfortable. I squirm a little as he goes at it and I roll my eyes. Just a regular fuck, then.

Halfway through my head gets cornered on the wall. I can tell he's getting close so I try to readjust so I can enjoy it. I keep worming down but get pushed back up. Finally I get my knees up between us and he stops. He's panting and sweaty; I'm covered in his sweat.

"Do you mind?" I say. "My head hurts."

"Almost done," he says and tries to get back in position.

"Not me," I say. I want to get back on top but he won't let me. He tosses the pillows and blankets on the floor then drags me down, too. As he's going my shoulder rubs the carpet, and soon it stings from the burn. He pushes up and pins my hair under his hand, tugging my roots so hard my eyes sting. I bite the insides of my cheeks and press my thighs together because I just want it to be over with. I know he's not the stopping type.

Then, from under the door, a shadow of someone rushes by. A door slams—it must be Casey's—and something drags across the floor. Heavy boots pause outside our door, and I think for sure someone's coming in. I try to lift my head to get a better look but my hair's caught in Rudy's fingers and I curse.

"Stop, okay?" I say and tilt my head. I try to push his arm off my hair but he's about to come and he's not paying attention. A man's voice trails down the hall, and then Casey's voice. I think I hear her say, "fuck off," then a chain rattle. My arm flails and I knock the beer over. It rolls under us and spills out over the blanket.

"What the fuck—"

Rudy starts and pulls away, fumbles for the can. I scramble up and try to peer out the peephole of the door. I can hear him finishing off behind me, hunched over on the floor. I grope for my underwear. I'm done. This wasn't what I'd hoped for; if I wanted a night like this I would have gone home with someone I knew better.

"You're on your own," I tell him.

He tells me I'm a bitch. I don't think that's fair and I almost get back down there and prove I'm not, but there's something weird going on next door and I want to see what it is. I crack the door open. Outside of Casey's door is old Boots-and-Shorts. He's got one foot in her room but she must have the chain locked. He rattles the knob. He's talking about her tits and whatnot. She can't stand that stuff and I know she must be really pissed off because she yells at him and tries to slam the door.

"Mate," I say, poking out a little farther. "She's not into you. Get going, right?"

Rudy flips the light on. I'm only in my underwear so I slam the door and scramble for the flower blanket. I don't want him to see me in the nude, not now. I sit on the bed and collect my clothes, pull my shirt and pants on and stuff my bra in my pocket.

I think I hear Casey call my name through the wall. I open the door.

"Gina?" she calls. "Don't go, okay? Are you still there?"

"Yeah," I call back. I glare at Old Boots. I remember him now, from the Hideout when I'd go with my dad. He used to harass the barmaids then, too, and no one much liked him. He's definitely banned, and I think he even went to jail for a while.

"You're not supposed to be up here," I say.

"I paid for a goddamn room like everyone else. Mind your business or you'll get some, too."

"Do it then," I say, and push the door open. The blanket and sheets are rumpled on the floor and Rudy's on the bed tying his shoes. For a second I wonder if he'll beat the guy up, but as he stands and pushes past me into the hallway, he catches Boots' eyes. He pulls his shirt on then puts his hands up as if to say, don't mind me, and takes off down the hall.

What a prick. I don't care. I can handle it. If Boots wants to take me I know Casey'll go down and get Mitch or someone quick enough. Then he definitely won't be back.

He grabs his crotch over his shorts and looks like he's going to either take me up on the offer or kick Casey's door in, but then he lurches forward.

"Cunts," he says in my face, close enough that his beard touches my lips. I pull back and he stumbles off.

I go to Casey's room. I slide my arm in and unlock the chain. What a bad idea, letting those guys stay up here with her. She's on the far side of the room. The bed is askew as if to bar the door.

"S'okay," I say. I'm about to suggest that we go down and get a beer and forget all about it but she looks pretty rough. She's all flushed and her hands shake.

"What the *fuck*"—she picks up a shoe and whips it past me into the hallway—"is wrong with this place. You're all freaks."

"They're just worked up," I tell her. She's had some rough nights here but I've never seen her this mad. She laughs.

"That piece of shit would have killed me if you hadn't been here."

"The door was locked," I remind her.

"Gina," she says. "You're so delusional. Don't you know you're practically raped every night of the week?"

I shake my head. This is beginning to sound familiar and I don't want to go through it again. I tell her to shut up.

"Even your parents don't want to be here," she continues. "Did you know that your dad paid Mitch McBride to protect you before he left? And I'm not going to be here to look out for you in a couple of months."

"Stop it," I tell her. "Just shut up, Casey." She sounds just like my old man and I want to punch something.

"I don't have time for this," she says and pushes past me. "I have to get back to work."

Downstairs I order three middies from Tam while Casey isn't looking and drink them on the far side of the bar, away from Mitch. When I'm done I don't want to stay here anymore.

Outside I trip along the dusty highway. I punch a road sign and it feels good so I punch it again. Casey pretends she's worried about me but it's her job to get me drunk and she always does what she's supposed to. She's so good at her job. I want to tell her that so I start to cross the road back to the Pony before I remember that I don't want to be there anymore tonight. I decide to sneak into the pool because I don't want to run into my parents, but then I remember they're gone.

I turn up the path to the trailer. The lights are off. I kick my shoes off and stumble through the kitchen. Joel and Marley are probably getting it on in our parents' room now that they have the master suite. I flick the light on in our room and see Marley's mound in her bed. I flick the lights back off and stumble toward her. I squint to make sure she's alone. I collapse onto her and drape myself backwards over her thighs. She startles.

"What the fuck?" She pushes me off, but lets me lie next to her even though the bed's a single.

"What's wrong?" she asks.

I sniff. I reach down and pull my bra out of my pocket. The underwire snaps and jabs me in the thigh. This was my only good bra. I try to push the wire back in, then give up and toss it on the floor.

"Who'd you sleep with?" she asks. She doesn't sound judgmental so much as worried for once. I don't say anything. My knuckles are wet and sticky.

"I'm glad they're gone," I say, dropping my head back on her pillow.

"You're being selfish," she says.

"He tried to strangle me," I tell her. I close my eyes. I'm spinning. "When I came home last night he was drunk and he started yelling at me. He choked me."

I hear a sob. It doesn't sound like me, but I know it is. Before I can stop myself, I'm telling Marley how our old man figured I'd been sleeping with one of his friends from the mine and when I came home he kept bugging me about it. I tried to shut our bedroom door but he came and grabbed me and pressed his thumbs into my throat long enough that I was scared.

"It was dark," I say, "but I spotted Mum in the hallway and she didn't stop him."

Eventually he let go and lumbered out of the house, slamming the door. Later, Mum came in with a bag of peas wrapped in a tea towel and told me to ice it so there wouldn't be a bruise, and that was it.

Marley's quiet for a while. I put my knuckles up to my face and touch my tongue to them. The blood is drying. I realize she's crying beside me.

"I didn't know."

"S'okay," I say, and I mean it. "It's not your fault."

I want to hear her say they're not ever welcome here, but she doesn't. She cries quietly then wipes her eyes on the sheet. We lie like that for a long time until I hear her breath change and I know she's falling asleep. I don't want to go to my own bed.

"Marley?"

She stirs and looks at me.

"I can't sleep. I've got the spins."

She sits up and rubs her eyes and then gets up with me. We go out to the kitchen and she grabs me a beer from the fridge and fishes a pack of cigarettes from between the couch cushions. I almost tell her off for smoking like I always do, then decide not to. It's been too long of a day.

We sit outside on the lawn chairs and look at the stars. The moths batter the screen door like they're trying to get in. That's *our* screen door, *our* kitchen. We own something. I look over at Marley and smile.

"Fire's closer," says Marley, sniffing the air.

It's true; somewhere in the distance smoke is coming in on the wind. I think of the sheep and wonder if they're being rounded up, and where the blaze is now.

Eventually Marley puts her half-smoked cigarette out in the dust and flings the pack into the bush. We sit there for a long time listening to a truck or two in the distance, somewhere far off on the highway, and the rasp of crickets. Every once in a while some ash flutters into our hair.

# GREYHOUND SPECIAL

4

BAD COFFEE can only keep you company for so long at four a.m. in a bus depot. Eventually I had to pick up and go. The taxis were all lined up there in the perpetual northern dawn. I hated to disappoint them as I passed by, lugging my guitar and cheap tent. It was probably all those cabbies had, that late-night bus straight out of the wilderness, but I was broke.

The campsite was far across town where the river curved and the highway headed out to nothing. It was okay to walk. I'd been cramped up on that bus since I parted with the band in Vancouver three days ago. I thought my legs might have splintered and come apart if I'd had to sit any longer. The only standing I'd done was in gas station alcoves, trying to occupy my fingers with pocket lint, my mouth with small talk instead of with cigarettes. Cigarettes were clogging my lungs, making my voice too raspy. Everyone decided it was time I thought about quitting and I couldn't disagree. But I'd broken down somewhere outside of Hope and bought a pack. I'd smoked my second-to-last one the night before in the bug-crazed darkness. The very last one had gone to an old Native guy worse off than me. Cold turkey, that's the way I thought was best. It didn't stop me from checking my jacket every three minutes, no, it made the habit worse. There I was in the mountain air with the sun coming up strong and cool at an ungodly hour and all I could think about was a smoke.

I'd been a little jumpy since I left Vancouver on the Greyhound. I'd just finished a cross-country tour with the band and we had planned on heading back to Toronto to recover and write some new music for an album that was long overdue. It was half-done. Everyone had been waiting for me to finish it so we could record. They were probably hauling ass somewhere in the prairies by now, taking turns behind the wheel, and maybe some pills to stay awake. We'd been on and off the road for the last two years and we were dying to get home. But for some reason, the morning we were supposed to leave, I had shoved most of my stuff in the van, grabbed my guitar and ended up at the bus depot in the middle of town. I'd called Lee and left a message to explain why I wasn't there. I didn't know how he had responded, because I'd turned off my phone and hadn't checked it since.

The guitar pulled my shoulder until it ached and I stopped at a bench as soon as I reached the river path. The sun was a strange beast. It was only five a.m. and there it was, crawling up the dome of the sky. I wanted to be horizontal but couldn't find the energy to remove my pack and lay my head down, so I got up and just kept walking. The river was a slow-moving sheet and I wanted to dunk my greasy mane in it until I noticed the deceptive undercurrent.

When I reached the outskirts of the campsite I turned onto the dark path of the long-termers. I passed impressive set-ups: tables of nailed and crooked branches, water jugs, clotheslines, tarps taut and firewood stacked. A small child with ratty hair watched me walk by as she licked honey from a spoon. I gave a half-committed wave but her eyes just kept steady somewhere above my head. It was dark in the dense pines. Fergus had lived here last year, or kept his clothes in a communal tent, anyway. The band had followed him back one night to grab some weed after a show. I'd called him three days ago to tell him I was coming to the Yukon. No big deal, I said. But it wasn't no big deal to him. The band had skipped Whitehorse this year and Fergus seemed choked up about it. He was quiet on the phone and it took me a minute to realize he wasn't annoyed. No, he was touched. Just do me one favour, I'd said. Don't tell Lee you heard from me.

I settled for a site somewhere between the big field and the long-termers. One of the sites tucked off the path, backing the river trail and a bridge. I unpacked my tent in the dust and discovered the poles were brittle old straws. I cursed as the tent creaked and threatened. I stood back. The structure was the most pitiful piece of shit I'd ever seen. It would fit half a child, maybe. I'd be spooning my guitar like a hard-curved lover every night and I wasn't sure what I'd do if it rained. I glanced at the sky and asked for a day or two to figure things out.

I wandered to the office. A sign read, "Open at 7 a.m." Firewood was ten bucks per load and you had to cut it yourself with a hundred-year-old handsaw. Families were starting to wake up and saunter bleary-eyed to the wash hut. I needed a shower but couldn't be bothered. I'd forgotten to pack soap anyway and I didn't have any change for the showers. I sighed and wandered back to the campsite, picking up sticks along the way. When I got to my site I ripped up the stub of a bus ticket and threw the wood on it. The fire was as pathetic as my tent. It smoked and smoldered and occasionally produced a lick of flame. Eventually a German in army gear came up and laughed at my fire.

"Pretty shit, hey?" I said.

He produced a fire-starting brick from some magical pocket and held it out.

"Oh, no, thanks," I said and shook my head. "I have to figure it out myself."

His eyes roamed my makeshift shithole and my guitar unveiled in her case. She was an especially beautiful guitar. I'd played her every day for the last twelve years. She was heavy, strong-boned and broad. My fingers knew exactly how to move over the frets. Whenever I picked up Lee's guitar, or someone else's, I was clumsier.

The German shrugged and wandered back to a picnic table to play cards. It's possible those were the first words I'd spoken since we'd passed the Welcome to Yukon sign the day before. The smattering of small talk on long, lonesome bus rides wasn't the same as in the city, I'd discovered. People liked to look right into your soul and say things like, "Girl, whatchyou running from?" or "I've met you before, yup, I know by those eyes." If it wasn't that, it was nothing at all. Somewhere along the line the talkative ones had disappeared back into the northern junctions.

That last night travelling through the cold northern summer had been the strangest. I was completely alone. I hadn't been alone in years, or at least that's what it felt like. I'd sat near the back of the bus and watched the shapes of people's heads against the windows, sneakers in the aisles and legs draped out. There wasn't a streetlight or sign of civilization for an hour or so, and then slowly the sky had lightened and the land had formed texture again. I'd seen mountain goats with wild tufts of fur, a moose outside a diner, and a brown bear and her cubs galloping with the bus. But it was the bison I had loved the most. They reminded me of Lee. He loved that kind of shit. Through the immediacy of the landscape, I realized how far I'd travelled and how impulsive I'd been.

I was tired. I went back to the office to pay for the campsite. The girl at the counter asked how long I was staying and I said I didn't know. I'd thought about it the whole way on the bus, but hadn't come to any conclusions. Part of me hoped I could just hide out here forever.

"You get a discount if you pay for a month," she said. "Twenty bucks off."

I eyed the chocolate muffin in the display case and felt for my wallet.

"Alright," I said, trying not to think about whether or not it was a good idea.

I trudged back through the campsite, passed a girl brushing

her teeth and cut through a soccer game. I walked right on through, unzipped my tent and collapsed headfirst with my boots half-out.

◈

When I came to, a dog was sniffing my armpit. I flipped over and saw a tall man's silhouette outside.

"Fergus?" I called.

"Dana." His face appeared and he grinned. I tried to sit up but my shoulder grazed the top of the tent.

"How are you?" he asked. He had a way of making casual conversation sound important. Like he really, really wanted to know how I was doing.

"Fine, man." My hair caught on the zipper as I manoeuvred out. I told him it was great to see him and gave him a big hug. It *was* great to see him. We hadn't spoken much over the last year. He was more Lee's friend, but he'd come to one of our shows when he was in Toronto a few months ago and we'd let him crash until he had to leave. He was likely the biggest music fan I'd ever known. He appreciated music like an old bottle of Scotch.

"You still out in that cabin in the woods?" I asked. Rumour had it he'd spent the Yukon winter without running water or electricity. I reached out and patted his dog, a carcass-thin husky. "This is your dog?"

"Yeah," he said absent-mindedly. "No, I'm not living there anymore. I've got a place over the river. It's decent except for my roommate. He's a little cunt, pardon my French."

I shrugged. "Cunt's a cunt."

"Do you want to move in? I've been looking for an excuse to kick him out."

I looked down at my set-up and realized I'd just spent most of my savings on a square of dirt. Maybe I could go back to the office and beg for my money back, take it one day at a time. But it was easier this way somehow. I was stuck here. I was committed. I would have to live the month out in this pathetic home I'd constructed, away from the city, unreachable. If I lived with Fergus I'd end up on the couch every afternoon strumming the guitar with the TV on mute until night came and we started drinking. I might whittle a song or two on the odd day of focus, but otherwise the month would be as good as torched. I didn't need distraction right now. I needed to figure out what the hell I was doing here.

I couldn't explain it to Fergus, so I just said, "Thanks, man, really. But I'm too broke and I don't think I'm staying long."

He shrugged, bent down and tumbled his dog into his arms before he insisted on taking me to lunch.

We drove to a bistro in the hills overlooking Whitehorse and sat on the patio built around thin pines. Fergus ordered us meat-thick sandwiches and glasses of beer. I was starving and fidgeted with a napkin while we waited for our food.

"How's it feel?" he asked.

I wasn't sure what he was referring to exactly—being in the Yukon, running away from Lee and the guys, or the general burn-out—but it was weird, all weird. Fergus's dog roamed the dusty parking lot with her nose down. I wondered how much Fergus knew about the band. We'd been on tour for a while, and didn't tend to keep in touch with anyone on the road, but if anyone would it was Lee. Maybe Fergus had heard all about how we'd been putting off the new record, or how everyone had been scattered and distant from each other these last few months. The drummer had met a girl in Montreal and was always jumping for the pay phone at pit stops, the bassist had a hard time staying sober enough to do the job right, and Lee and I, well, I guess our hearts weren't in it like before. Lee hinted it was me, that I wasn't as reliable or enthusiastic as I used to be, and maybe in some ways it was true—wasn't everyone changing all the time? But I'd seen it in his eyes, too. He didn't know how to keep it up like before, when it was mostly just me and him in our shitty Toronto apartment, working kitchen jobs so that we could come home and write music all night.

Mainly I was just tired. I'd been waiting for a chance to relax, just a month or two. But the record was long overdue; our label had been hounding us for a year now, and it was my job to come up with the skeletons of the songs because that was how we'd always worked. I'd tried to explain it to Lee, but he didn't seem to believe me. It was like he thought there must be something fundamentally wrong with me, that it was all so serious.

The beer arrived. I ran my fingers over the condensation before taking a small sip. I'd planned on abstaining for a while, thought it might be easier up here in the Yukon. I realized that would not be the case. No, in a strange land booze chased you all the more.

"Do you have a smoke?" I asked.

Fergus shook his head. I ripped the corners of the coaster until it was shredded, then leapt up and wandered around the side of the building. The cook was at the kitchen's back door tossing a butt into a can. No milk crates for this classy joint.

I bummed one and wandered around the thin trees. The nicotine melted my insides. Even the guilt of caving and the nagging concern about my voice slid away. Everything would be okay. The world would be saved, one cigarette at a time. I pulled in, savouring everything about it.

I ran my hand down the bark of a tree. I'd read there were forests just before the Arctic Circle where the trees were only as high as my hips and thin as my arms but were over a hundred years old. If you cut one down you'd hardly be able to see its rings because of the density of the wood. It was the permafrost or something. You had to admire them. Maybe if I stayed long enough I would make it up there and see for myself. No one would dream of finding me there. I coughed and spat in the dirt.

Our sandwiches were on the table when I got back. Fergus had picked at his but as soon as I sat down I started to devour mine.

I couldn't be polite about it; I was starving. I'd been living off corn chips and scotch mints since I boarded the Greyhound in Vancouver and it wasn't like I'd been eating well before. I took a gulp of beer.

"Sorry," I said, as I shoved the bread in my face.

Fergus picked at his sandwich like the bird that he was. He didn't seem to notice how hungry I was, or he was pretending not to notice. I forced myself to pause and sat back to look at my friend.

"There's a jam party out near Miles Canyon tonight at my friend Simone's," he said.

"Jam party," I said.

"Yah, you know." He slipped a chunk of sandwich to his skinny dog and she tasted it gingerly. "Can I sign you up?"

"There's a sign-up?" I asked.

"No, but you know what I mean. Everyone's excited to hear you play. Miss Dana Soule of Old Dollar Bill."

"I don't know, man," I said. I'd kind of been looking forward to not being a musician for a while and just being a weirdo in a tent on the river.

He sniffed and picked up his beer, sat back.

"How's the music coming, anyway?" he said.

"You've been talking to Lee," I said, feeling defensive.

He didn't say anything, just sat back with his hazel eyes trans-fixed on mine in that intense way of his. I couldn't tell if he was hurt I didn't want to play, judging me or compassionately waiting for me to spill my heart out. I squinted at him and he didn't flinch, didn't even blink. I sighed and rubbed my eyes with the heel of my palm.

"I can't write songs anymore," I admitted.

Fergus shrugged. "You'll do it."

I shook my head. I wanted to tell him that was an arrogant thing to say, that he didn't know my situation at all, but I stopped myself. He meant well. I scratched the soft wood of the table with my nail. At some point, I wouldn't have hesitated to whip out a pocketknife and etch a profanity there, but those days were gone, so gone.

I looked up and caught him dead in the eye.

"I just don't know what it's going to take," I said.

"Just play tonight," he said, as if that would solve all my problems.

"Okay, fine."

Fergus looked pleased and took his first big bite of sandwich. Then he leaned forward and winked. "If you need anything else, just let me know."

"What do you mean?" I pulled a strip of smoked meat from my plate. I got the impression he wasn't talking about food or music. I grinned and pretended to look around. "You've got hookers hiding somewhere around here?"

Fergus dropped his head and smiled. After all the time I'd known the man I still couldn't tell if he was shy or just pretending.

"Remember when I came to Toronto last year? When I got back I hitched from Lillooet and these guys picked me up."

"Yeah?" I realized he wasn't going to finish his story. "What? You gave them blowjobs?"

That got one of his shy headshakes.

"They had a business proposal for me."

"Uh huh."

"There's a market up here. The competition is bad."

"Uh huh."

"All I'm saying is that if you need anything I probably have it," he said. "Also, you know, I'd like to treat you while you're here. I know you don't have a lot of cash and money doesn't mean the same to me anymore."

I dropped my eyes and nodded. It was true; I was flat broke. The only way I'd get my money from the tour was if I rolled back into Toronto soon. I knew Lee wouldn't wire it to me. He was too smart for that.

"That reminds me," Fergus said. "You're going to love my friend Simone."

"Yeah?"

He nodded.

"But does she like girls?" I was skeptical; it was always good to be skeptical.

"Oh yeah," he said.

"Fergus."

"Just, she does, okay?"

When Fergus sauntered in to pay the bill I caught myself wondering if he was dealing to the restaurant staff on the side. I bent down and tried to pet the anorexic dog but she dodged me.

We drove back to town and Fergus had a couple of stops to make. I wasn't in the mood to play hitch-around-with-the-dealer so I jumped out and promised him I'd wander over in the evening for the party.

I criss-crossed through town trying to memorize the streets. It didn't take long to walk from edge to edge. I found a bakery and ducked in for a loaf of sourdough. I'd heard there was a glorified convenience store at this edge of town and I cut down another street to find it. There were huskies all over the place. I bent down and patted them as I passed. They were panting and tufts of hair came off on my fingers, even though the sun wasn't hot, just high up there and endless. A man on a tiny BMX circled the block. He looked like he should have been twelve but he must have been at least forty-five. I bet he had a DUI and this was his only way of passing time. I gave him a nod before pushing the glass door open.

I wandered the aisles and marvelled at the price of food. Nine bucks for a carton of orange juice. Five for a pack of pasta. Peppers were twelve a pound. My eyes widened. I thought about slipping a brick of cheese up my sleeve but couldn't. I found myself between the liquor and a cooler of beer. I almost picked up a bottle of whiskey to bring to Fergus's, then forced myself to keep walking. I'd be broke by the end of the week if I started that up. It was better if I kept clear-eyed. I wasn't on vacation.

I grabbed a jar of peanut butter and made my way to the front counter. As the lady counted my change I caved and added a pack of Belmonts to the total and pulled the rest of my change from my pocket. I was short thirty cents and I wouldn't have any coins for the shower unless I went to the ATM but I couldn't stomach the service fee and besides, if I had cash I'd spend it like it was air. The lady waved me away, saying I could owe her the rest.

Outside the old BMXer had circled his way to the far end of the block. A chick stood at the pay phone speaking an angry type of French. I eyed her. I knew I should call Lee. It was the decent thing to do; I knew that. He was like family and he might be worried about me. At the very least, he'd be pissed right off at me and that was fair, too. I owed him a phone call if only so he could lay it all on me.

But I couldn't. That would be too responsible, too thoughtful. Maybe I *was* the Dana Lee saw in me. I passed by the phone, promising myself I would make the call tomorrow. I caught the girl's eye and got a lump in the throat. I hoped this was the Simone of the jam party, but knew it probably wasn't. I tried to look casual as I shoved the plastic from my cigarette pack into a trashcan but my heart quickened. I glanced back and saw her watching me. I knew some French from weekends in Montreal. I tried to conjure up a sentence or two as I dipped down to the river path.

"As-tu du feu?" I muttered under my breath, realizing my dirty habits might be as deep as my French went.

At the campsite I pulled my guitar from the tent and wandered down to the river. There was a long footbridge that I knew led to Fergus's place and I sat under the blue arch with my feet in the frigid mountain pools and sang as soft as I could. I played songs I'd written years ago and let myself enjoy the familiarity of them. Eventually I gave up trying to be quiet and just played into the deep acoustics of the steel and water.

◈

The sun still shone at nine that night as I walked over to Fergus's. I didn't think it would ever stop impressing me, that sun. It was even brighter and more relentless farther north, I'd been told. We'd been to Dawson for the music festival the summer before but I couldn't remember being in awe of the sun then. I guess I hadn't slowed down enough to really notice it. Fergus's place was just outside town. The bugs got worse the farther I walked. Soon my face stung with mosquito bites.

His place was some sort of low-grade townhouse. I knocked on the door and when no one answered I pushed my way in, discovered a split-level staircase. I followed the stairs down to a door and knocked again. This time a kid with stoner eyes opened it. He didn't ask me who I was; he just wandered away, leaving the door open. I wanted to ask him if he was the infamous cunt I'd heard so much about but I wasn't sure it was even the right place. I inched in when I noticed Fergus's shoes on the mat. I slid mine off next to his before the skinny dog vibrated in, then slinked away from me.

"Fergus?" I called.

The apartment was a living room, a kitchen and a hallway with a filthy bathroom and two closed doors. I heard Fergus's murmurs through one and knocked softly. He opened the door just wide enough to push his face out. Behind him I saw a girl's legs and another dude's shoes on the floor.

"Hey, man," he said. His eyes were red-rimmed. He fished through his pocket and produced a set of keys. "I'm just in the middle of something. Take my roommate's car. I'll meet you at the bar in half an hour."

"Your roommate's car?" I asked, but he'd already disappeared back into the room. "Which one is it?"

I stood in the hallway for a few minutes feeling awkward. I put my face right up to the roommate's closed door and spoke.

"Is it okay if I take your car? It's kind of weird."

The only reply was the clicking of a keyboard. I wandered out to the kitchen and picked at some cold beans on the stove before going back outside. I presumed the car was in the back parking lot so I wandered out there and stood in front of half a dozen vehicles, each as beater and unsuspecting as the next. I studied the key for a clue but found none. I sighed and walked over to the first car. It wasn't locked so I'd have to actually get in and try the ignition.

"Fuck me," I said and searched the back seat for signs of Fergus's stoner roommate.

I didn't have the guts, so I walked over to the next car and peered into that back seat. There was a box of Kleenex and a silk scarf. I crossed it off the list. The next one was a huge truck. The key seemed too dainty to belong to a truck that big. The next car was locked. I glanced at the row of windows in the townhouse. They all seemed to glare at me as I slid the key into the lock. It got stuck and I had to jiggle it out. The alarm blared into the evening. I sighed and turned to face the houses with my hands up in surrender. Eventually a guy wandered out frowning and I tried to smile. A girl trailed behind him. I recognized her legs as Fergus's company, and sure enough he was next to round the corner.

"Sorry," I said. I said it again as the guy pushed his key set at the car.

"It's in front. The red one," Fergus said, wrapping an arm around me. He turned to the guy. "This is my friend Dana."

The guy nodded in my direction with a vague look of disgust. He and Fergus talked low for a while. I stood off to the side, Fergus's special, androgynous little sister. Eventually I went out front and sat in the passenger seat of the car and waited.

That night Fergus and I drove out to what I can only call the boonies. We blared music the whole way, flailing and dancing in our seats. When we turned onto a dirt road, Fergus lit a joint and passed it to me. We passed it back and forth until the sun almost seemed to dip away for once behind the spindly forest. The car crawled along the dusty driveway and Fergus's nose hung over the steering wheel.

"Kinda creepy," I said.

Fergus straightened up and grinned. There were parked cars in the distance and then people, and beyond that an open shed crammed with more people and their instruments. I could hear the pierce of a crappy amp and stuck my head out the window.

"Here." Fergus tossed me a bottle of bug spray.

"This shit'll kill you," I said and flung it on the dashboard.

"Suit yourself." He rubbed it into his arms and slapped it on his face.

I stepped out and was instantly coated with mosquitoes. I hopped around, slapping them, my skin already stinging. I tried to pull my shirt lower down my arms, but then lost shoulder coverage and cursed. I took a deep breath and told myself to go somewhere Zen, that tonight could be punishment for all the bad shit I'd done lately.

I found Fergus talking to some people and wandered over. He wrapped his arm around me and they all grinned.

"Hey," I said, giving a little wave.

Fergus pointed at his friends and rattled off their names. "Dave, Brandi, Ola, Mickey and Simone."

When he pointed to Simone, his arm froze as though he thought I might not understand the significance of the introduction without a full minute of obviousness. I pushed his arm down and gave him a look.

"Dana," I said quietly, and everyone nodded enthusiastically.

I glanced at Simone. She wasn't the French chick I'd seen on the pay phone earlier, and when she turned to talk to Ola I was disappointed to realize she just had a French name. But it didn't matter. She had small, articulate hands that moved a lot when she spoke, and creamy skin and dark hair. I stared for a while until she turned to me and I blinked and looked away.

"So you're on the run," she said.

"No, no," I said, then laughed. "People keep asking me that. Is that the only reason people come here?"

She laughed and shrugged. "The further north you go, the worse it is."

"Alaska is full of fugitives," I said.

"Thieves."

"Rapists."

"Serial killers. All of them."

I looked around. There was a tall farm-type house with all the lights on and a calmer kind of music coming from within. People wandered in and out. It was a pretty sight. Beyond that was a yard of sorts, and the jam shed where the feedback continued to give some long-haired guy at the microphone grief. All around was a strange kind of forest. Sticks of trees that radiated a chalky white in the Yukon dusk.

"Nice place," I said. Mosquito bites puffed my face. Maybe soon they would bite every last inch of skin and there would be nowhere left and they'd have to leave me alone.

"It's my parents' house," she said. "We do this every year."

"They don't mind"—I pointed to the shed where the shrill sound came from—"that?"

She smiled. "I guess not. All their friends are in there getting drunk and playing acoustic anyway."

Fergus led us to the jam shed and we jumped around for a bit until I got pushed into the crowd and forced to the microphone. When I started singing the party cheered. I laughed. So this was how Yukon folk got down. It didn't take much to impress them, and for some reason that was all right.

◆

Fergus and I fell asleep in the front seats of the car that night. We'd had the sense to pillage some blankets from the trunk before we dropped the seats and passed out with our mouths open. When I came to it was impossible to tell what time it was, what with that beastly sun glittering in the trees. It was dead quiet and the ground outside looked cold, so I figured it must be early.

Outside, I wrapped my blanket around my shoulders and wandered through the yard to find somewhere respectable to piss. The strange white trees seemed to go on forever in a half-committed attempt at a real forest. I walked until I couldn't see the house. I was groggy and wanted to sleep more, then remembered my shitty tent and felt depressed. I hadn't been in my own bed in months, and even then I couldn't remember really sleeping in it. Passing out, definitely. Sprawling, yes. But a good long sleep? It had been a while. "I'll never, ever take you for granted again," I whispered to my bed in Toronto.

As I walked back through the trees I grappled with the urge to rouse Fergus and tell him to put me on the first plane eastward. The stubborn part of me wrestled the weak part until I noticed a man on the porch lighting a cigarette. He waved me over. I got closer and realized he must be Simone's dad. He grinned a red wine mouth. He obviously hadn't gone to bed yet. I glanced through the screen door. A group of old-timers was still up in living room.

"Come on in, come on in," he said and waved his arms around.

He shuffled in looking pleased with himself. The ash from his cigarette dropped on a thread-thin Persian rug.

"Barry!" a woman squawked from an armchair. "Get that filthy thing out of here or else pass it around!"

Everyone chuckled.

"Hey," I said. "I was just, I slept in the car—"

"Get her a cup of coffee, Barry," the woman said, putting her feet up on the coffee table. "Her, right? Her?"

I ran a hand over my wild blond mane and nodded.

"You play the piano?" someone asked.

"Not really," I said. I had, I could, technically, but I never did.

"Great," said the woman. She reached behind her for a string instrument I couldn't place. She jabbed Barry's cigarette at the piano bench. "Sit there and give us the melody and we'll all jump in."

Someone poured a glass of wine and Barry came back with a steaming cup of coffee and picked up a guitar. I sat down and ran my fingers over the keys. They weren't dusty, and for some reason that surprised me. I always expected pianos to be dusty as hell. I played a couple chords, then turned around to look at the old-timers.

"I'm not really into the piano," I said. "I'm better on the guitar."

Everyone erupted in a disappointed groan.

"Honey, we're all better on the guitar. Just play."

I gritted my teeth and turned back around. I stared at the keys for a moment, then reached out and tried one or two. I cleared my throat and played some simple chords until I got the hang of it. One by one they all jumped in with their different instruments. I wished Fergus would come in and save me, but here I was, with musical savages, forced to play. I glanced behind me. There were several guitars, the strange string instrument, a harmonica and some bongos. Eventually the woman started singing along and I had to admire her for that. She hardly missed a beat, even if you couldn't really decipher what she was saying. When one song wound down, someone else would strike up another and we went on this way for a while until I noticed Simone sitting on the stairs to the second floor. Her hair was knotted up on one side and it made my heart jump. She waved. When we were done, Barry grinned at me.

"Hey, she's pretty good, isn't she? She's pretty good."

I shrugged. "I'm in a band in Toronto."

"We know who you are!" someone piped in.

"Who is she?" someone else asked in a low voice.

"The lead singer for Old Dollar Bill!" said the woman. And

they struck up one of the band's better-known songs, all together, and it sounded so awful I caught myself grinning.

◈

Later that afternoon I took a nap back in the tent. When I woke sometime later after a troubled sleep I was nearly suffocating in my private sauna. I opened my thick-tongued mouth, paralyzed under the sleeping bag I'd for some reason decided I needed. When I found the strength to move my damp limbs and rip the door open, I couldn't tell what time it was and that gave me an eerie feeling. It could have been five p.m. or ten p.m. I had no way of knowing, so I rummaged through my bag, found my cellphone and stared at the blank screen. It was time to turn it on. There was probably a pile of messages and texts.

"Dammit," I muttered and flicked it on.

I held my breath as it warmed up. The screen read seven in the evening. I waited for the endless vibrations to start, half dreading it, half excited. But there was nothing. I flicked through my texts; nothing new. There might have been a couple missed calls but no messages. I dropped the phone in my lap. It was a strange, fucked-up feeling to have fled to Yukon Territory without a word of warning and to find that *no one* gave a shit.

I got up and found the water pump. I stuck my mouth under it and tried to work the handle at the same time and ended up with water up my nose and somehow down my sleeve. I cursed and looked around the campsite. What a hole. What had I gotten myself into?

I decided to walk to Fergus's place. I was starving so I ate a hunk of bread smeared with peanut butter while I walked. Hopefully he'd have something better to eat. Some mayflies flipped their bodies against my eyes and I blinked like an idiot, then eventually gave up and just got flies in the creases of my eyelids and along my cheeks.

Fergus's door was locked. I knocked quietly at first, then louder. The TV murmured through the crack under the door. Skinny Dog's claws clicked along the floorboards and then stopped. She was probably standing a millimetre from the door, smelling me, laughing at my misfortune. I sighed and sat on the stairwell. It was dark down there. A washing machine churned behind another door, and a pot crashed from somewhere else. I got up and wandered outside. I didn't want another parking lot incident, but I sure as hell wasn't ready to head back to the tent and whittle away the evening alone. I tried to walk casually, but not overtly, along the back windows of the building. Fergus's apartment was below ground and I peered down into his kitchen. I knew it was his because I saw Skinny Dog at the door where I'd left her, and I could see Fergus, the bastard himself, passed out on the couch.

"Fergus," I hissed through the screen. The window was open a few inches.

I touched the screen and decided it would be simple enough to pop it off and jump right in. I glanced up, looking for witnesses. No big deal, I thought.

Skinny Dog scattered when she saw me in her kitchen, right by her food dish, in the sanctity of her home. She disappeared in a nervous fit down the hallway as I replaced the screen. There was some crusty pasta in a pot and I picked at it until it was all gone. There was almost nothing in the fridge. I opened the cupboards and found a can of minestrone soup that looked like it was from the eighties, and some organic protein bars, the kind that cost like three bucks each.

"Who are you?" I muttered and stuffed one in my mouth.

I plopped down on the couch across from Fergus's. Dog hair and dust spewed into the air. The evening sunlight came slanting in, blessing the underground cave. Fergus didn't wake up, didn't even move. He breathed too loud so I reached over and turned up the volume of the TV. I watched some crappy show until I decided I was probably the biggest piece of shit that had ever lived. Here I was doing exactly what I didn't want to do, wasting away my youth, wasting away my talent, torching my life one day at a time.

I got up and paced the room, then grabbed the cheap guitar against the TV stand. It was dusty and too light and flat, but I tuned it the best I could and strummed. I played and scrawled some lyrics on the back of a magazine and played some more. I was pissed off, and the more I played the madder I got, and the worse I felt the quicker the songs came out.

I was getting somewhere when there was a knock at the door. I glanced at Fergus, but he didn't stir. I tried to ignore whoever was there, but they'd obviously heard me playing and I couldn't ignore them unless I was quiet. I sighed and got up.

"Hello," I said to a dude when I opened the door. I recognized him from around town. He looked like a big dumb dog, so eager.

"Hey, man," he said, tucking his hair behind his ears. "I'm Bruno."

"Bruno," I said. I couldn't keep the smile down.

"I heard you, you're really good," he said, pointing at the guitar in my hand.

"Oh, thanks," I said. I glanced back to see if my friend was awake. "Um, you're here for Fergus?"

Bruno nodded.

"Fergus," I said, then tried again louder. He cracked an eye, then rolled over to push his face into the cushions. Oh, so that's how it was.

"He's sleeping," said Bruno, nodding. "That's okay, I just need a dime bag. I'll wait."

He pushed past me and jumped onto the other couch. He grabbed the remote and notched the volume.

"Wank," I muttered to Fergus as I collected the scraps of paper I'd been scrawling on. The music would have to wait for today. It was just as well; it was better to quit while you were ahead than to dry up. I told Bruno I'd best be on my way. I gave Fergus a jab in the arm and told him to call me when he was done pretending, then took the stairs out two at a time.

◈

Outside the campsite office I picked up the pay phone receiver and pressed 0, then Lee's number. It rang several times and I realized he might be asleep. It was a lot later in Toronto and he was a bit of an early riser. I was about to hang up when he answered.

"Yourworstnightmare," I said quickly into the collect call prompt. He couldn't turn me down; he'd done it to me lots of times. I heard him chuckle as he accepted the call.

"Hi," he said.

"Hey." I dragged my foot through the dirt. "I'm in the Yukon."

"I know," he said. "My call display says YT."

"Oh."

"Nah," he said. "Fergus told me before you even got there."

"What a cock," I said. That Fergus. What a guy, real one-of-a-kind.

Lee took a deep breath like he was going to say all the things he'd ever needed to say. I got ready to get my fight on, but he didn't speak. So he would take the high road. He would chastise me with silence. Neither of us spoke for a long time.

Finally he said, "You're wasting my money."

"Fuck," I said and slammed the receiver down.

I stood in the strange twilight of the north for a few minutes. Moths battered the orange porch light of the office.

"Fuck," I said again and punched the metal siding of the pay phone.

I picked up the phone and dialed 0 again.

"Sorry," I said into the prompt, and after a few excruciating seconds he accepted the call. But, again, he didn't speak.

"Okay," I said, trying to get my shit together. "Okay."

My mind raced. I could tell him I was coming home tomorrow. I could accept that I was being selfish and just recommit to everything, work through the anxiety of writing music. I could even tell him I was terrified of failing, of letting them down. But it all left a weight in my gut. I knew nothing would change, even if I was honest with him.

"We've been nominated for a Polaris Prize," he said. "Ricky says we have a good chance. He says it's almost in the bag."

I didn't say anything. Papers rustled somewhere in the universe as Lee cleared his throat.

"'Dana Soule,'" he said. "'Dana Soule's heart-wrenching lyricism and haunting vocals make Old Dollar Bill one of the country's leading alt bands. Lee Brennan's signature country-blues-style guitar and electric blends combine to create an unshakable sound.' It goes on for a while."

My knees weakened. A giddiness fizzed up. It was huge; the biggest acknowledgment the band had ever gotten. I held onto a piece of it and let it feed my ego for a moment before the inevitable anxiety returned. We'd been waiting for this for a long time. But what we'd never talked about was how it meant no end in sight— that we were all as good as hitched and shacked up together. I might as well wear a gold band to ward off any temptation. Funny, I'd never anticipated the commitment. There used to be nothing easier, nothing better than playing music with the guys. Now it required discipline and schedule.

"What are you doing up there, Dana?" Lee asked.

"Thinking," I whispered.

"We have interviews lined up as early as next week," he said.

"Okay," I said.

"Okay?"

I ran my fingers down the etched numbers on the phone.

"I'll call you tomorrow," I said and hung up gently.

I ran to the river path. My Chucks slapped the pavement. It did not feel good to run. No, it felt awful to run. My hair did not fly behind me and I did not feel the cool mountain breeze on my face. My limbs seemed to flap in different rhythms and directions. I passed a cool-looking couple strolling, passing a beer back and forth. My skin got damp and hot and my lungs wheezed. The worse it felt the harder I ran, like I was punishing myself. The river glazed by in the opposite direction.

Finally, I let myself collapse on the bench at the edge of town. It was the same one I'd sat on that first morning in Whitehorse. This time I leaned back, let my arms drape over the sides as I heaved. I couldn't move for fear of puking on myself.

Finally, when I felt half-decent I dragged myself up and walked to the convenience store. I walked straight to the back section and grabbed a mickey of whiskey. It was all I could afford. I hesitated and put it down. I picked up a huge bottle of red wine, appreciated its heft for a moment, then put it back too. Whiskey would make me mad, and that might be nice. But it might not be enough to do the trick. My fingers trailed over the bottles. The wine would knock me out and it would get me nice and sappy, maybe even sentimental, and maybe that was the healthier choice. I picked it up again, once more impressed with its weight. But it would hurt so bad in the morning, more than the whiskey. I put it down.

"Tough call," someone said.

I looked up. Simone had a bag of chips and some five-dollar celery and was watching me from the next aisle. I blushed.

"If you get the wine, I'll share it with you," she said. "Might help ease the pain."

It was settled, then.

We walked to the footbridge by my campsite and swung our legs over the edge. My guitar lay beside me at Simone's request. It was almost dusky out and the bugs explored our skin as we passed the bottle back and forth. It felt good to have company. The deep pit of anxiety about the band had been replaced with jitters from sitting beside a beautiful chick and I appreciated the distraction. I glanced at her. I liked how her hands gripped the bottle. They were strong and delicate. She tilted the wine back. A stream of wine escaped her lips and trickled down her neck. She reared forward and sprayed the wine out into the oblivion of the river and laughed, wiping her collarbone. I laughed too.

"Hey," she said. "This doesn't taste half bad if you spit it out."

"Lemme try," I said and took a swig, then pursed my lips. A fountain of wine arched out over my legs. We laughed, half-hysterical, our cheeks flushed. We passed it back and forth, making up new ways to spit wine for a while, then went back to just drinking it.

Before long I had my guitar in my hands and was trying to remember the songs I'd written earlier. I played a few chords and sang softly, trying to match the two up, but kept stalling. I couldn't get it to flow like earlier. Maybe they were all shit and I just hadn't noticed. I sighed and put her down.

"Aw," said Simone.

I shrugged. The wine was acidic in my gut now. I couldn't concentrate on the instrument. I put my chin on the railing and swung my feet back and forth. I knew I had to get my shit together and quick but I didn't know how.

I couldn't stay here, but all I wanted was to climb farther and farther north, into what I could only imagine was oblivion. I glanced at Simone. Maybe she would come with me. We could hide in the hip-high forests of the Arctic Circle and learn how to grow old in shallow, stony ground. But what did that even mean? Simone passed me the bottle and our fingers touched. I didn't know how to resist temptation; I'd never learned. Maybe that's what made Lee so nervous. He could see it in me all along, knew I would crack under pressure when it really started to count.

I gripped the bottle by the neck. It was still heavy, even though it was only a quarter full. The glass itself was heavy. My hand was just heavier, maybe, now that the wine saturated my blood. Before I could think about it, I reared my arm back and whipped the bottle outwards, into the dusky air, and it careened down into that soft steel river that seemed to flow counterintuitively, pulling the bottle in the opposite direction, under the bridge and away. I stared at Simone and she stared at me, then we looked out over the water without a word.

The next morning I woke up in my half-collapsed tent in my clothes. My lips were cracked and dried. I tasted blood on them. I lay with the A-frame of the tent an inch from my face for what felt like an hour. I had to leave. Today. Now. But I couldn't move. The longer I lay, the worse it felt. Tiny stones pierced my back. I reached for my pockets hoping to find a smoke but didn't. Served me right. I pushed the tent away from my face and realized I was snug against my guitar. She was probably all out of tune. I gave her a strum and realized there was a piece of paper shoved along the frets. An address was scrawled on it almost illegibly. I didn't recognize it. I gripped my head. Had I been there? No. I had a vague sense of Simone talking about meeting me somewhere but couldn't pinpoint it.

Finally I got up. My head spun in the cool air and I sat right back down at the picnic bench. The collapsed tent flapped in the breeze. One of the poles had finally given in. I wanted to cry. I was ripe with self-pity. But I held it in as I packed up. I didn't bother to fold the tent, just whipped the poles into the firepit and tucked the billowing piece of shit under my arm. I walked clear across the campsite with my pack, my guitar in tow and my tent destined for the dumpster.

The office bell chimed as I pushed through the door. My eyes were cloudy and my hands shook. I needed food and a cup of coffee or else I might die.

"Listen," I said to the chick behind the counter. "I only stayed a few nights."

"We don't usually give refunds," she said, glancing toward the back room.

"Please," I said. "Please, man."

The clock ticked behind her on the wood wall and flies buzzed along the window frames. I sighed.

"At least give the next person who takes my site a break," I said. "It's paid for until the end of the month."

She glanced down at her book and clicked a pen. Then her eyes brushed over my filthy black T-shirt and my wine-stained, bloody mouth. She jabbed the cash register, counted out a few bills and threw them on the counter like she didn't want to have to change her mind.

"Two weeks' refund," she said. "Don't tell anyone I did it."

"Shit, thanks." I grabbed my guitar. "Thank you."

I shoved the cash in my pocket and got out of there.

I found Fergus in town, sitting back at a café on Main Street with his sunglasses on and a toque pulled over his wild hair. I threw myself down beside him and grabbed his hat and tossed it on the table.

"Too fucking hot," I said. I was in no mood for his eccentricities. Skinny Dog eyed me from under the table, her ribs working hard.

"Where you going?" asked Fergus, glancing at my stuff.

"Home."

He let the newspaper drift down and gave me his full attention.

"But you just got here."

I shrugged. "I miss Eastern Standard, I guess."

He thought about that. He took a sip of coffee. Then he got up and disappeared inside for a while. When he came back out he had a big plate of breakfast and coffee for me. He put it down without a word. I was simultaneously repulsed and relieved to have food in front of me. All my resentment of Fergus slipped away as I took a mouthful of hot coffee. He pushed his sunglasses up and watched me with that intense gaze of his.

"You really have to go?" he asked.

I nodded and fingered some egg onto my toast. I told him I'd talked to Lee last night and it was time to get my ass back to reality. The thought of that reality made my stomach flip. I still didn't know how I was going to manage it, but I knew I had to.

Fergus sighed, slapped his paper down and crossed his arms. He looked pissed off but I couldn't be sure. Finally he looked up at me.

"Let me buy your ticket home," he said. "I owe Lee for something. There's a flight once a day—you can take the one tomorrow morning and throw it down with me tonight like old times."

I nodded. It was a generous offer and I didn't know how to say no. It sounded all right, more than all right. Besides, I didn't have much choice. But my stomach flipped with more than just a hangover. This time tomorrow I'd be face to face with Lee, the guys and a never-ending itinerary. The truth was, I was tapped out, shrivelled, and it wasn't going to change just because I was home.

I remembered the paper I'd found shoved under my strings and handed it to Fergus.

"The studio?" he said.

"I think Simone left it for me last night."

Fergus raised his eyebrows. I shrugged.

"It's right behind us," he said. "In the alley."

I jiggled my leg under the table until I knocked my coffee and made a mess.

"Go," said Fergus, waving me off. "It's fine. I'll be here all morning. I've got business. Leave your shit."

I grinned and grabbed my guitar. I told him I'd see him in an hour or so, but he'd already pulled his toque back on and picked up the paper.

◈

I found her stooped over an old box camera in the studio in the alley. I lingered in the doorway for a moment, not sure if she'd heard me arrive. She was fiddling with the aperture. The camera was fixed on a big white wall. There was a stool and that was all. The only light came in through the storefront window. It was all so minimal it made me nervous, choked me up a little though I couldn't tell why. I leaned my guitar against the wall.

"It's hard without a light meter," she said, startling me. "Most of my photos turn out grey but I like the process."

I nodded. I couldn't think of anything worthwhile to say. Her hair was pulled back and her face looked different. She looked clear and light. I touched my hair and realized with horror that my wild mane had decided to tangle into a dread on half my head. How could she look so good? I felt like I'd been ravaged.

"I'm heading out tomorrow," I said, and she finally turned around to look at me. I shifted on my feet, self-conscious.

"Yeah," she said. "You told me last night."

"I did?"

She nodded. "You kept saying you were going to take the Greyhound all the way back to Toronto."

I scoffed before I realized she was serious. I gaped at her and she grinned, amused.

"You don't remember?" She laughed. "What else were you saying? You said you were going to get it all figured out through, what was it, self-induced confinement."

I burst out laughing and she joined me. I shook my head and rubbed my forehead. I was a riot. I told her Fergus was buying me a plane ticket home tomorrow and her eyes widened.

"Are you sure?" she said. "You seemed like you were having some kind of epiphany or something."

"Goddamn." I tried to remember the conversation but just couldn't. "There's no way."

"It's ridiculous," she agreed.

I sighed and slumped down the wall. How many days was that? Too many. I'd either have to head all the way back to Vancouver and then east, or else cross through northern prairie for god knows how long. I shuddered. My legs ached just thinking about it. I looked up at Simone, half-pleading. She laughed and shrugged.

"It was your idea," she said. "There's even a special on right now. You could probably get there for like a hundred bucks."

I coughed. I had a little over a hundred in my pocket from my campsite refund. I groaned and rubbed the heel of my hand into my eyes. She was right. I was right. I needed to take the Greyhound for an excruciating length of time. It was the only way.

"You want to come with me?" I asked before I could stop myself.

"Fuck, no!" She was grinning, trying to spare my feelings.

I wanted to ask if it was more me, or more the week in a filthy bus across the prairies, but suddenly it didn't matter. I would see her again, somehow. Besides, it was for the best. I need to be alone, bound to myself, before getting back to the band.

Now, I focused on the cross-country trip. I was summoning stamina. I could do it. I would do it. And something would happen between here and there. Gods knows what. But it was bound to happen.

# ONCE IT BREAKS

**JUNE STRINGS** the coral above the boat's kitchen sink and it hangs like dried flowers. She doesn't like that her husband brings it home. The coral comes up in his salmon nets fragile and white, and he's not supposed to take it but he always does. Once it breaks it's dead, he reminds her. But he takes so much, hands it out like carnations.

Two days ago the coral was everywhere—white branches in girls' hands, piled next to kids with their stick rods over the dock—and she knew he was home before she spotted the *Mayfield* towering over the working dock. She'd been at the beach with the kids and when they saw the boat, Jasper and Minke took off down the planks, calling him, but she didn't follow. She climbed onto the forty-foot sailboat they called home and sank into the dim cavern below. The coral was waiting on the kitchen table. She picked it up. A peace offering, maybe, or else meant to taunt her. Jonas's intentions were like a shadow show: all she saw was the effect.

Now, she fingers the brittle gift above the sink and it tinks on the window. It's pretty in the sunlight, but she'll only leave it for a few days to avoid a fight, then she'll slip it back into the water. The coral belongs in the ocean, dead or not.

The boat is so quiet that she's uneasy. Jonas took the kids out for the afternoon, probably to the General for ice cream. He asked her to come, but she couldn't. The kids watched as he wrapped his arms around hers and whispered in her ear. She shook her head, barely looked him in the eye. Feeling like a cohesive family takes longer and longer each time he comes home. She can't tell anymore if they're better off together or apart.

She sits on the kitchen bench and runs her dry palms over her face. No, she can't enjoy the silence of the boat, but it's not just Jonas. Her friend Hannah passed away three weeks ago, just a few days after Jonas left on the *Mayfield*. She hasn't mentioned it to him, hasn't even explained to the kids. No one asks. She'll have to tell them soon—the funeral home will call about the ashes—but right now her sadness is muted, like the beach stone in her sweater pocket. She would have to remove it, show it off, for anyone to notice.

Hannah was sick for as long as June knew her, a year and a half at least. Her death was like a slow-moving barge, heavy and obvious. She'd refused every type of treatment, accepting only the odd healing session from an artist friend. She let June bring homemade soup and change the sheets toward the end, but she withheld the cancer from most acquaintances. Jonas was gone most of the time, and the kids watched on in the hallways of Hannah's house, sat in the hot car when Hannah's appointments ran late. Maybe they knew how she'd grown apart from them during these last few months. She morphed suddenly into someone separate from their needs, catering to something more desperate, more urgent. They watched Hannah grow gaunt and brittle. After Hannah died, June looked up one morning to notice that their milk teeth were pushing in adult teeth, their chubby legs growing lean. She was taken aback, as though the two events were braided.

June flips through the address book from Hannah's kitchen drawer. The names and numbers are scrawled out like Hannah never intended to call any of them. Some are alphabetized by first name, some last, and some seemingly at random. It is perfectly Hannah. June's throat tightens when she finds her own name in the J's.

She was caught off guard when the phone calls came on the odd afternoon. Why her? They were little more than acquaintances; their art hung in the same group shows from year to year, and they made small talk over plastic cups of wine and cheese cubes at openings, but they weren't friends. Hannah didn't seem to have friends, but then again, neither did June.

June sighs and drops the book. What will she do when the ashes come? No family left. There's an ex-boyfriend somewhere, but she can't track him down. An art acquaintance heard he's in Australia, but another thinks he committed suicide last year.

Jasper and Minke pound down the dock. The boat rocks. June tosses the address book into her purse and blasts the dishwater. Their giggles float above her. Down the ladder, Jonas brushes his hand against her hair, half tender, half accident.

Later that afternoon June has boxes to deal with at Hannah's. She can't find Jonas or the kids on the dock. She wanders up the ramp, shielding her eyes, then spots them on the far edge of the marina. There's Jonas on the *Mayfield*, cracking a beer with a buddy while the kids fish nearby. Jasper isn't wearing his hat and his nose is peeling from yesterday. Minke is without her lifejacket and teeters on the edge of the dock to scrape mussels from below the oily water line. June sighs and rubs her forehead.

She turns toward the parking lot, keys in hand, but she already knows she won't leave them. He isn't even watching them. He's back for one lousy day and he's already given up pretending. He laughs at something his friend says, and June crosses down the planks, anger rising. Even as the heat flushes up her neck she knows she doesn't have the energy to remind Jonas that Minke can't swim, or that Jasper gets sunstroke. She doesn't have the patience to teach the kids, again and again, to look after themselves when they're with their father. Besides, nothing bad could possibly happen to them with Jonas. He doesn't believe in children drowning or crushing their arms between a massive fishing boat and the dock. They're safe with him.

She stops at the edge of the last dock where her children play, where the wind picks up and the whitecaps chop the distance. Shiner scales and boat fuel fill the air, and oily mussels crush in the heat. She stoops to pick up Minke, barely four, and brushes shards of shell from her knees. She bends down and pulls up a cluster of mussels for Jasper. She draws a hand over his forehead, pushes his hair back. He's already burnt.

Hysteria doesn't work; she knows that. If she doesn't protect them calmly, quietly, then they'll turn on her. She looks up at Jonas but he doesn't notice her. She catches his friend's eye and tries to keep her face neutral. Self-control gives her something Jonas can't, though it's lonelier this way.

"I'm taking the kids," she calls up to him. "I have some errands."

"I'll watch them. Let 'em stay, they're having fun."

June takes a deep breath and lets it out. "I think they've had too much sun."

"So you're going to stick them in a hot car?" He drops his beer and jumps down.

She squints at him. He's only thirty-five, but he has fisherman skin: dark red, and lines cut around the eyes from squinting over the water. His beard is scraggly and too long. She used to love how he was wild, delinquent. Somewhere, deep down, she is the same as him, but she can't fit those pieces of themselves into marriage or parenting; she's tried for years and it can't be done.

"I'm organizing Hannah's house." She drops her eyes. "I'd like their help."

"It's not good for them," he says.

"Jonas."

"It's a beautiful summer day."

She glares. She almost blurts that Hannah is dead, but Jasper stands and leans against her. He's tired. Too much sugar and sun.

"Bring a book or something," she says, refusing Jonas's eye. Minke writhes in her hands. June tightens her grip. Since when is Minke so strong?

"I want to stay," she cries.

"No," says June. "You can't be here alone."

Minke flails and June grips her, tries to hoist her up. Minke's foot catches June's shin. The heat of the day pushes through her. She's a bad mother, she knows that, as bad as Jonas and maybe worse. But she heaves her daughter over her shoulder. She tries to keep a calm face as she passes him.

Halfway up the ramp her bag slips from her shoulder and hangs in the crook of her arm. It's heavy. These two loads are too heavy, but she keeps walking right up the ramp, past the tourist licking ice cream, past the small children shedding lifejackets at the washroom, and Minke cries the whole way.

Hannah's house is down a long dirt driveway in the bush. A couple of acreage houses glimmer through the pines, then Hannah's one-bedroom bungalow with a grassy yard, deer fence and forest. The sandy garden beds are empty except for ancient kale stalks going to seed.

June parks and the engine tinks in the heat. She doesn't move. The kids haven't been here in a while, not since Hannah moved to the hospice. It's weird, bringing her kids to a dead woman's house, June can see that now.

"Is Hannah here?" Jasper asks.

"No." June swivels to face him. "No, sweetheart."

She'll tell them before they leave today. They'll say goodbye to the house together. Minke kicks the back of June's seat, her little foot thumping over and over again.

"I don't want to go," whines Minke.

"There's the rope swing," says June. "You can't stay in the car."

By the time June unlocks the front door, her kids have swung their doors open, dangled their feet in the dust and peeled themselves from the back seat.

The house is stuffy. June pushes the windows open. She wanders the rooms like she has every time since Hannah died. She's managed to box some linens and dishes for the thrift store, but there are things she'll never know what to do with: Hannah's intaglio prints in the back shed, letters and a few notebooks she hasn't opened and probably never will. How can she be left with these things? Some days it feels like a cruel joke.

At forty-two Hannah had never married or had kids. She was airy and introverted, which accentuated her aloneness as friends dropped away to start families or careers. Only Hannah's intensity kept her on the ground, unlike June, who feels like she could sink and never resurface. When Hannah told June about the cancer, she looked tired deep, deep down but her eyes were bright.

"I asked for it," Hannah said.

"No," said June.

"It's okay," she insisted. "I asked for a challenge and this is what I got."

When she refused treatment, June was never sure if Hannah thought she would beat the cancer, or if she just wanted to go with some dignity. She devoted herself to cancer. Only toward the end did she start to crack.

June opens the fridge. There isn't much: a sediment-heavy soup, a container of miso, some pickled ginger and a carton of baking soda. She grabs a bag from under the sink and tosses the food in, then drags the fridge a few inches from the wall. She gropes for the plug in the dark, cobwebbed corner. She sighs as the fridge whirs down, then she pulls herself onto the counter.

The kids bicker somewhere in the yard, but she can only see the dense forest from the kitchen window. How would her family manage if something happened to her? She slips a hand into her shirt and cups a sweaty breast. Maybe she has cancer, too. She tries to remember to look for lumps in the shower, but sometimes months go by, and sometimes she can't tell what's normal or not.

Sometimes she thinks about leaving Jonas, or at least what it would look like to leave. He wouldn't be surprised. Or maybe he would. She used to worry about him. He was gone so much, for so long. If he called one day to announce he wasn't coming back, she wouldn't be shocked.

But if she ever left Jonas she'd have to leave the ocean. She would walk down to the boat to pick up the kids after his weekend visits, lead them home to a small house on the hill to cook dinner on a full-sized stove. It might be better. But she would never sleep properly again, no; land meant a hard-slat sleep no matter how tired she was, no matter how soft the bed. She'd rather go down to the desert, Joshua Tree or somewhere outside of Vegas. She'd rather sleep in a trailer under a huge desert sky and wake up every morning to a red dust earth and nothing but cratered landfills or military remnants. But the kids wouldn't fit there. She's thinking of another woman, another life. She'll have to wait; she'll have to die and make different decisions next time around.

In the kitchen June slips a number off the fridge. She's been dreading this all week: the call to Hannah's landlord, Margaret. She spoke to the woman the day after Hannah passed away. After her sympathies, Margaret gave June a gentle deadline. By the end of July the house had to be empty for a new tenant. She could arrange a donation pickup for the larger items, but otherwise she hoped the house would be sparse. June holds her breath as the phone rings.

"June!" Margaret exclaims when she picks up. "Tell me, how is everything?"

"Well," says June. "It's fine, but there are things. I don't know where to put some of the more important things. Like the art. It's in the back shed. I was hoping someone from her artist group could store it at the gallery, but I haven't heard back from anyone."

"Oh dear," says Margaret.

There's a long pause. The last thing Margaret wants is a dead tenant's remnants cluttering up the house.

"I would take it, but I live on a boat," June tries again.

The landlady sighs. A pen taps somewhere on the other end.

"Leave it," she says. "We'll deal with it later."

June peers out the window to catch a glance at her kids but they're not at the rope swing. She pulls the phone away as Margaret rambles about the maintenance man, but she can't hear them either.

"He'll be by tomorrow," says Margaret. "He'll paint the bathroom and kitchen."

"Okay," says June, but her heart jumps. She wanted a few more days at least. She says goodbye and hangs up. Without the whir of the fridge, the house's silence is overwhelming, louder than seems possible.

Outside, the sun slants and ducks behind the forest of pines. She scans the yard, then the driveway, then again. After a few dumb seconds she realizes her children are missing. She turns around but doesn't see them. She looks in the car, half expecting to find them napping, but it's empty, one of the doors left swung open. She calls for them, but knows they won't answer. It's too quiet; they've been gone for too long, she can tell by the stillness. But she calls again, and then again. Her voice is timid at first, then billows out into the forest. Please, she thinks.

She runs to the deer fence and discovers it's flimsy and passable. She squeezes through. Dry pine needles and dirt fill her sandals. She yells for Minke, then Jasper, but she knows they're not out there. The stillness in the trees terrifies her. There isn't even bird-song. Her heart pounds in her ears as she runs through salmonberry and salal toward the neighbours. A dog barks in the distance, more alarmed as she nears the house, but she can't stop. She pounds up the stairs to the door and bangs on it, catching her breath. Whoever answers the door will think she's a bad mother, but she can't search alone. She can't be everywhere at once.

But no one comes. She stands for a long time and catches her breath. The wind chimes ring in the garden, a bus barrels down the highway in the distance. She grips her forehead and frowns away hot tears. She can't think straight. She could be running around these woods until the sun goes down, half-blind and frantic.

Down the driveway, June stops at the dusty fork in the road that leads to the highway or to Hannah's house. She doesn't know what to do. She calls their names again and again.

"Answer me." Her voice, strange and unfamiliar, bounces through the trees.

Then, she's afraid to be alone. She takes off down the drive-way toward the car. She could get in and drive down the high-way, calling for them, until she reaches someone to help. But she knows she can't do that, knows she can't leave. She finds her phone on the passenger-side floor, spilled from her purse, and calls Jonas. As it rings, she realizes he won't pick up. He won't pick up no matter how many times she calls. His phone is prob-ably at the bottom of the boat, forgotten in a pile of clothes or on a dark bathroom shelf. He's not there because he's never there when she needs him.

"Hello?"

She chokes when she hears his voice.

"I need you to come to Hannah's," she says. "The kids are gone. I can't find them."

"Okay," he says. "Okay."

She explains where the house is and sobs when she hangs up.

She's useless and pitiful. Her adrenaline is gone and now she just feels pathetic.

She walks down the driveway and tries to keep her eyes sharp on the trees. She calls for them and strains to hear their voices, but there's nothing. She could call the police. All the horrible things that could happen to them: bears and cougars and coyotes down from the mountain; kids trapped in neighbours' basements for decades; the ones who are never found.

June stands at the end of the driveway in the late-afternoon sun. Is it her fault? Of course it is. Cars whip past her every once in a while and disappear down the long forest highway. Minke and Jasper could have come out here. They could be a mile down the road, bleeding in a ditch somewhere. She covers her mouth and looks up at the sky. Somewhere, thousands of feet above her, a jet trail forms in the blue.

Then Jonas's truck is there, slowing to make the left turn into the driveway. She steps aside to let him pull in and hears their voices, sees their heads with their bobbing haircuts low in the passenger seat. They're excited, wild. She watches, stunned. The truck lurches as Jonas parks and swings the door open. They call to her, their voices so high and sweet. She catches Jonas's eye, but she doesn't understand. Her children clamber out of the truck behind him. They talk all at once, but she's too numb to understand. Her knees shake and she drops, holds her arms out. Minke runs up, lets herself be hugged, then pulls away.

"Where were you?" June asks.

"We went for a walk on the road," cries Jasper. "We got lost, then Papa found us."

June's hands shake. She drags them over her face. How could she be so stupid, letting them wander off to the highway where anything could have happened? She looks up at Jonas, half-pleading, expects him to be smug or relieved or at least as baffled as her. But he doesn't seem to notice. He's ready to head back to the dock, his work here done. She stares at him, wants him to look at her and acknowledge her terror, but he doesn't.

"I just don't understand," says June. Her family stares at her. "What were you thinking, walking out to the highway alone?"

"We were bored, Mama," says Minke.

June scoffs. Jonas cups his large hand over his daughter's head. "Let's go," he says.

"No," says June. "They can't just disappear like that."

"Told you not to bring them here," he says.

"So that makes it okay?"

Jonas shrugs. Her relief sours to frustration. Why is she always the one to carry the weight? What would happen if she didn't care anymore? Everything important would slip through the cracks, like the space between the docks where the fishing line tangles and snaps and stays forgotten. Good, she thinks. Let it.

She towers over Minke and wants to hurt her, and Jasper, dragging his sandal in the dirt, oblivious. June digs her nails into her palms. She wants to slap them, grab their soft arms and shake them until they remember how important she is. She wants to knock love into them, grip them until they feel sorry for her, for everything that's gone wrong.

June turns back toward Hannah's house. She doesn't want them to see her cry. She tells them to go home without her and the truck revs. Crickets cling to dry grass stalks under the pines. It's not late, just after dinnertime, but the sun is disappearing between the slats of trees around the property. On the boat, where nothing clutters the horizon, there is sun for an hour or two more. Tonight the tide will be high, swelling under everything. The sky and water will be some majestic colour, almost a joke, like peach or lilac. Tonight it will be so beautiful that no one could overlook it, not even Jonas. Not even Minke or Jasper.

June kicks her sandals off on the porch. The house dims as evening fades, but she doesn't turn the lamps on. In the morning the maintenance man will paint over the walls. He'll stir up the air, confuse the remnants of Hannah right out. June will leave her key on the table and load the rest of the boxes into her trunk for the thrift store. There won't be much point in coming back after that. She'll put Hannah's notebooks and private letters with the art and call the new tenant once in a while to make sure the shed roof isn't dripping and the windowsills aren't moldy. Maybe the gallery will organize a memorial show sometime in the fall and she can help transport the pieces to a framer, sort the prints by the years and themes.

June opens a box in the hallway and pulls out some bedsheets. The red armchair in the corner of the living room reminds her of Hannah, even though she never saw her sit there. Maybe she'll take it, store it somewhere in case she ever has a use for furniture. She tries to ignore the rest of the pieces: the ratty couch, side tables, kitchen chairs, the framed landscape on the wall by the potbelly stove. These things will stay with the new tenant, or disappear at the dump, or maybe one day she'll come across them in the thrift store when she least expects it.

Down the hall, Hannah's old bedroom is darkest. She catches her reflection in a mirror above the highboy. She hasn't had a long, hard look at her face in ages. She looks away. Her body is a mother's body—her stomach misshapen, sacrificed. Somehow that never bothered her.

June covers the mattress with a sheet that smells both washed and used. All the pillows that propped Hannah up are gone; June tossed those first. The blankets are packed somewhere in the car. She slips her shorts off and drops them on the floor, then climbs onto the bed. She lies back and puts her hands on her hipbones. Without a pillow, her body seems to tip backwards. She closes her eyes, slightly dizzy. The mattress is old and too soft, as uncomfortable as she expected.

Hannah's last days in this bed were the worst. Before she moved to the hospice, June found her lying here, bare legs twisted in the sheets as she sobbed. June told the kids to wait outside and they fumbled off quickly, knowing something they didn't understand. She stood with Hannah and tried to talk to her, but she was unreachable.

June wipes her eyes and folds her arms over her face. She'd tried to forget about that day. She wanted to remember Hannah barrelling toward her fate, knowing whatever happened was inevitable but that she just had to be present; she just had to face it for everything to be okay.

But she failed, didn't she? Hannah broke too soon, fear ravaged her, and June is failing at life. Besides, Hannah is gone. Even if her art molds in the back shed, or June scatters her ashes alone some quiet afternoon, Hannah is still gone. June can't change that just because she's here in the house, just like she can't change how her children lose their milk teeth, or that she suddenly doesn't know how to love them. She can't change that Jonas disappoints her, or that she disappoints herself. Nothing can change it now. All the rot is already there, below the surface, like Hannah's cancer. June rolls onto her side and watches the window's fading blue as the heat of the day radiates from her skin.

# SUNG SPIT—PART ONE

THE BEACH HOUSES along Sung Spit were built on hundred-year land leases. No one really owned them, and in the years before the leases ended the tenants abandoned the cabins one by one until the last few dwellers were told to leave. The cabins had already been empty for a few months the summer my cousin Kendall and I discovered them. Some of the windows were sheeted with plywood, and boards criss-crossed the front doors, but most of the cabins were open and intact as though their inhabitants had stood up from breakfast and walked out, never looking back.

On a late June afternoon, Kendall and I met on the small homebound ferry. I'd just finished my last class of grade eleven and was overwhelmed by summer, the anxiety of groundless days. I felt like I might float away down the forest path through Sung Spit to be pulled and lifted over the overhang of the beach houses, over the rocks and up into the hot, blue sky. Kendall lived for that kind of freedom; she was a year older than me and more or less a dropout. She would have graduated at our high school's ceremony the following week if she'd stuck with it, but she hadn't even managed to make it in Alternative. She said she didn't care about finishing, but I think she did. I think she'd slipped too far behind, didn't know how to catch up, and was too proud to ask for help. Auntie Trish said she was bound for a rotten path and she'd better smarten up. She always compared us, saying I was smart to finish school and work part-time at Village Grocery. But that didn't help anyone. Kendall spared me resentment; she knew I didn't feel superior. She and Auntie Trish couldn't be in the same room without turning volatile.

When the local paper ran an article about the Sung Spit development and the abandoned cabins, Kendall and I knew we had to find them. They would be torn down within two years, but for now they sat empty. We'd stood out on the ferry car deck one morning, squinting at the shoreline as the boat swung out into the narrow passage to town on the main island. Sure enough, there was the row of cabins.

After the ferry, we rode halfway to Sung Spit with a neighbour and asked to get out just before the highway forked. We cut down onto a forest path where water glinted through the cedar boughs. Somewhere in the distance a motorboat puttered in the ocean, probably hauling a crab trap, but it didn't stay long. As we trailed down toward the shore, the peninsula opened to the desolate islands. We were almost completely alone on this side of the island.

Seven cabins perched there between the slim offering of forest and the ocean. We wandered around, peered through windows, into cracks in the boards. Eventually we returned to the first cabin and agreed it was probably the last abandoned because it was so intact. We walked up the crumbling steps and pushed the door. When it swung in heavy and our eyes adjusted to the dimness, we discovered a musty shag carpet littered with toys, an old tiled fireplace with paperbacks and a vase on the mantel. I stepped in first. Soft on the sagging floor, I studied every object and wondered who had lived here. I knew Kendall was behind me, already calculating how she was going to make it hers.

The carpet was thick like grass. An armchair sat by a window with heavy floral curtains. No tables or chairs in the kitchen, but the fridge and stove were still there, the cupboard doors open. The smell was just how you'd expect, dank and dusty, but with something extra, the alders outside maybe, the ocean yards away. The outside and the inside almost mingled.

Kendall crept in behind me and breathed out long and low, as though she'd entered a new habitat and knew just how to adjust. She tested the floorboards, jiggled on the soft wood. She kicked a soother out of the way and took a little jump.

"Don't," I said.

She grinned and hopped again.

"If it's going to collapse," she said, "we might as well get it over with."

I was beginning to understand that even if you tried to do all the right things, you could still end up damaged, bad at living. Kendall knew how, better than anyone I'd known. She didn't hesitate on the brink of things; she hurled herself through the days. I wanted to be close to her that summer, closer than usual. I knew she wouldn't be around much longer, and when she left she wouldn't come home on the weekends to do laundry and raid the fridge. I wanted to be with her for selfish reasons, too. I hoped some of her ruthlessness would rub off on me. I'd made some mistakes that year and was still trying to figure out how to reconcile with them, and how to be brave.

Kendall opened the cupboards to a few pots and pans, some plastic plates and sippy cups. She sorted through them, tossing the kids stuff in a pile near the soother. I went to the mantel and picked up the books. Turning the pages, wafts of dust and mildew made me sneeze.

"This place is kind of creepy," I said, but Kendall was engrossed in sorting the kitchen.

"Don't be a snob," she said. She had plans for the place; I could tell.

She'd run away to the city once. She was fourteen and said she'd stay with Russ, her dad. She crashed there for a week or two but eventually he called Auntie Trish to ask if Kendall was back home because he hadn't seen her in a while. Trish went nuts, threatening to get him arrested for abduction or child neglect, but by the end of the weekend Kendall was back, her hair black and septum pierced. She told me later that she'd ended up squatting in a condemned punk house in East Van with a guy she'd met. Tons of people did it, she said. There was a whole underground world we were missing out on. But she didn't go back.

Auntie Trish kept her on a tight rein after that, got the school counsellor involved and made sure she had structure and consequences. When she started to skip school again, they let her go to Alternative in the outbuilding next to the high school, but eventually she ditched that, too. I think the only reason she stuck around the island was that she knew Auntie Trish would track her down and make her life hell if she took off.

"Hey, Cassie," she said from the kitchen corner.

She'd swapped Cassiopeia for Cassie that year in an attempt to liberate us from our mothers' tastes. The hippy-dippy sisters, she called them, but I hated the name Cassie.

I looked up just as she turned with an outstretched arm and recoiled when I realized the stick in her hand held a thick, blue-grey ball of fuzz. I squealed and made for the door. What must have been an orange whipped passed me, barely missing my back. It landed on the stairs and rolled down to the beach with a puff of mold. She was still laughing when I slapped her arm.

"You're disgusting," I said, but she only laughed harder.

In the evening, we wandered back through the stretch of houses. Kendall had taken to the moldy seventies house, but I liked the shackled cabin at the opposite end. It was drafty and minimal. Hollyhocks grew beside the entrance—there was no door anymore—and inside the wood was bare and brittle. I stepped over shards of glass in my flip flops and looked around.

"This one is mine," I said.

"I don't care," she said. "You should bring Elliot here."

I reddened. I wasn't seeing him anymore, and she knew it. She wanted to know why I'd broken up with him over a month ago.

I'd lost my virginity to him around Christmas, but that was all she knew.

She could talk for hours about guys she'd met, all the nasty details, the dirtier the better. But I clammed up when she asked. Sex wasn't a joke to me; sometimes I didn't understand her. Once she told me she'd take him if I was done with him. I think she did it just to egg me on, but sometimes I tried to imagine them in bed together, what it would be like. I *was* done with him, so maybe it shouldn't matter. I told her to go for it. I don't think either of us knew if the other was joking or not, and maybe we didn't know ourselves.

That night Kendall and I split up where the highway forked. She had a longer walk; Auntie Trish had the old family cabin by the village. Kendall had a little brother, Lucas, whom she babied, and some half siblings in Alberta from her dad's other failed marriage, but she never saw them. Auntie Trish might have been waiting for Kendall when she came home wanting to know where she'd been, but my mother, Sadie, didn't care. Word got around pretty fast on this island. If you did something you shouldn't be doing, most of the time everyone knew right away.

I came in, dropped my pack by the door and asked if there was dinner. Sadie sat on the couch with the TV on mute. Ulla, her girlfriend's dog, stretched out beside her.

"You let the dog up?" I asked.

Sadie shrugged. "She was getting territorial about Pomme. I thought I'd try to woo her."

The dog weirded me out. She had anxiety problems and compulsively licked her back until it was raw. Pomme, my mom's girlfriend, didn't seem much better but at least she didn't look as gross. I sat on the arm of the sofa next to Sadie and the dog growled without raising her head. Sadie patted Ulla, but I could tell she was wary of the animal, too.

"How was your last day?" Sadie asked.

I shrugged. I'd lost interest in school last month but my grades didn't show it so no one really noticed. Sadie looked tired. I reached out and picked up a strand of her feathery blond hair. The toilet flushed down the hall and I went to the kitchen to fish my plate from the oven.

"Thanks," I said and nodded to Pomme in the hallway.

I heard them murmur and closed my door. They were always murmuring; it bothered me. I wished they would just speak at a normal level. There was always something wrong, some issue to discuss. Right now Pomme was probably insisting that I hated her because I hadn't smiled.

Sadie was different with Pomme than she'd been with boy-friends. She was careful with men, always warning me before she had them over for the night, making sure I felt comfortable with them. I liked them all fine and she was always so tentative that eventually I just said, "Sadie. I don't care. Seriously." But when Pomme came along, Sadie relaxed. They sat on the porch at dusk and smoked pot, or went to shows at the Hall. Pomme lived on an oyster farm on Stuart Island, a twenty-minute boat ride away, but pretty soon she'd found a way to stay over almost every night.

I sat on my bed and picked at the potatoes on my plate. I didn't have much of an appetite, but Sadie would notice if I didn't finish dinner. She might not say anything, but she would notice. Most of our food came from the garden and she took it personally if anyone wasted a scrap. I chewed but everything tasted strange these days. When I was done I unpacked my bag, still full from crap I'd stashed in my locker. I tossed my old gym strip into the laundry basket, made a pile of papers I wanted to keep, then changed my mind and tossed them all out.

Down the hall, the phone rang and Sadie appeared at my door.

"It's Elliot," Sadie said with her hand over the receiver.

"You're supposed to tell him I'm not home."

"I know," she said. "I just can't lie to him this time."

I frowned and grabbed the phone. I waited until I could hear Sadie offer Pomme tea in the kitchen before I answered.

"I just wanted to check on you," he said.

Elliot was a year younger than me but he'd skipped two grades over the years, so you couldn't really tell. He lived on our island but went to the other high school in town. I'd asked him not to call me since we broke up a month ago. Talking to him made our mistake seem too real.

"I'm fine," I said, then sighed and reached for my day planner. "I haven't gotten it."

I flipped back a few pages and looked at the big red circle I'd drawn. My period was almost three weeks late, but I'd known something was wrong before that.

"Do you feel anything?" he asked.

"No," I lied. Everything felt different. I just wanted Elliot to leave me alone. I didn't want to be with him anymore. I wanted to deal with it myself. It embarrassed me when he asked too many specific questions. If I were Kendall, I would know exactly what to say to him. I would know how to handle myself. I probably would have never gotten into this mess. Kendall started having sex when she was thirteen and she'd never gotten pregnant. She said she didn't use a condom half the time, but I couldn't tell if she was lying.

"I just don't want to talk about it anymore," I said. "I'll tell you if I need help."

I hung up and sat on the bed for a long time with the calendar in my hand. Eventually I was so tired I laid my head down and fell asleep with the light in my eyes and my jeans on.

I spent my first day of summer vacation working. I had a cashier job at the Village Grocery where I'd been part-time for a few months.

Now that school was out I figured I'd make as much money as I could between days spent tagging along with Kendall.

Kendall was supposed to meet me after my shift ended at five. We wanted to get to the cabins without anyone seeing us, but it was tricky. The walk took forty-five minutes, which I didn't mind, but Kendall refused. I figured we could catch a ride with someone we knew, pretend we were headed to the ferry and duck down to the abandoned cabins instead. Neither of our mothers had bothered to teach us to drive. Trish was too high-strung to let Kendall get behind the wheel and our car was always breaking down.

Outside the store, I waited a long time for Kendall and watched people come and go. I knew most of them but pretended not to notice. Ignoring every second person who passed took real skill. I saw my grade two teacher out of the corner of my eye, then one of Sadie's best friends, my manager, a girl I'd known since the minute we were born and finally my old piano teacher before Kendall came up, breathless.

"Let's go," she said and grabbed my elbow.

"I just saw Ms. Callahan. She lives by Sung."

"Nah," she said as we walked to the island's only intersection. "We've got to hitchhike. It's less obvious."

I shook my head and told her that couldn't possibly be true.

"It'll be fine," she insisted. "We'll be able to tell ahead of time if we know the driver. We'll just pretend we're walking on the side of the road if we don't want a ride from them."

"So we're going to accept a ride from a stranger instead of someone we know," I said.

"Yes, Cassie. We're going to take a ride from a stranger."

She smirked and I slapped her arm.

"Okay, fine," I said. "But no unmarked vans."

Out on the highway, the summer had shifted and it was just a grey, lukewarm day. It was depressing out there, squinting at cars as they approached. My heart skipped every time I saw one in the distance.

"Who's that?"

"Martin," I said. "That guy who works at the gas station."

She jabbed her thumb out. I asked her if she hitched a lot. It was my first time, but I didn't want her to know. She shook her head.

"Not on the island," she said. "Only in town." ·

"You thumb in town?" I asked. Town was full of rednecks and transients. I didn't like the idea of her hitching over there.

Martin from the gas station halted and stared over the passenger window. He was probably in his twenties, maybe older. He was kind of a loner. There weren't many guys his age on the island; anyone with any sense left when they could. I peered into his car. There were two-litre Pepsi bottles on the floor and just so much garbage.

"How's it going, Martin?" said Kendall as she leaned in. "Want to give us a ride?"

"I don't know," he said and turned toward his back seat as if he'd never seen it before. But Kendall had already opened the door and pulled the front seat back for me to crawl in. I shot her a dirty look as I pushed the seat clear. My first time hitchhiking and here I was in a back-seat dump with no escape route. At least I knew the guy. I stared at his profile and tried to gauge whether or not he could be a murderer.

"We're going to Sung Spit," said Kendall, ripping a piece of nail off with her teeth. She spat it on the floor. I reached for my seatbelt and tried to find the buckle amidst all the trash. Eventually I gave up and willed Martin to drive like a decent person. Kendall was telling Martin about our abandoned cabins.

"Hey—"

"You want to check them out?" asked Kendall, ignoring me.

"Why?" he asked.

"I dunno." She glanced back with a smirk. "It might be fun."

I shook my head and stared out the window. Whatever she was up to I didn't want to be a part of it. I was queasy from the back seat and curvy road down to the spit. There was a greasy smell back there. An old pizza box, maybe. I wanted to tell them to stop but I was afraid if I opened my mouth I might puke. I clamped my jaw and breathed through my nose. Finally, Martin pulled onto the gravel shoulder. We were still a ways from the path but Kendall jumped out and yanked the front seat back for me.

"Go without me," I managed to say.

"What's wrong?" she asked.

"Nothing."

I turned my back to them, feeling something rise in my throat. I heard them muttering but when I turned back they were in the distance, cutting down the forest path. I hunched over. Sweat burned my forehead. It was the worst feeling I'd ever known, that moment before vomiting. Finally, it came. I puked again and again, until my eyes went blurry. I fumbled back to the car and sat on the hood. I wiped my face as the relief of an empty stomach settled in. I spat on the road and pushed my hair back. After a few minutes, I felt so much better I almost grinned.

I wandered down the forest path and spotted Kendall and Martin on the beach, heads down. Kendall laughed. I hadn't heard that laugh before. I slowed and watched them. She had a lit cigarette between her fingers and so did Martin. They must have been his; she was always trying to get ahold of them and Auntie Trish was always confiscating them.

"I'm going to give Martin a tour of my seventies house," she called.

Martin shrugged and allowed himself to be pulled along.

"I'm going," I said, annoyed that I'd been dragged here. I'd walk back to the village if no one pitied me on the side of the road, then call Sadie for a ride. I was tired. I just wanted to go to bed.

"No," said Kendall, turning back. She jogged over and gripped my arms. There was a fierceness in her eye. She almost looked high, but I couldn't imagine what on or when she'd done it. "Don't go, please. We won't be long. Then Martin will drive us home."

I rolled my eyes.

"Please, Cassie."

"Don't call me that," I said, already resigned to staying.

"Okay," she said. "Okay. Wait here."

I heard her prop the door closed with something heavy, then nothing but the ocean lapping in and out. It was calm on this part of the island. It seemed strange that more people didn't live out here. It was warmer, more sheltered, and wilder. I guessed there would be more places soon enough once the houses were torn down and replaced with developments.

I shifted on my log and glanced back at Kendall's house, then heard Martin shout. He sounded surprised. I stood up. The door swung open and he charged out, spitting.

"What's wrong with you?" he cried and wiped his mouth.

I caught his eye and he just shook his head and disappeared up the path, his long legs powering up the hill. Kendall stood in the doorway with that old smirk on her face. I took the stairs two at a time.

"What?" I asked.

"I gave him a blowjob," she said.

I made a face. I guess I wasn't surprised, but that guy? "You blew Martin?"

She shrugged. "Then I gave him a taste of his own medicine."

"That's disgusting," I said. "You're disgusting."

"I thought he might like it." She shrugged. "I got his cigarettes. It's almost a full pack."

"Disgusting," I said again, and shook my head, but really, she amazed me.

The next morning at home I woke up with the sun just coming up over the treeline and the day seemed fully optimistic. I pulled my curtains back and watched the sun slant in through the cedars, warming the deck where the grapevine exploded over its trellis. I lay still for a while. A rhythmical sound rang from the yard, and it took me a few minutes to clue in. I sat up. Someone was digging. I threw on a huge T-shirt from the thrift store and padded down the hall. Sadie's bedroom door was ajar.

I found her standing on the deck with her hand over her mouth. She was watching Pomme, who stood beside the chicken coop with a shovel and wheelbarrow.

"What?"

She sighed and wrapped her arm around me.

"The chickens were attacked at dawn," she said.

"All of them?" I dropped off the deck onto the gravel driveway. We'd moved the coop closer to the house last fall after we'd lost too many to coyotes. During the day they roamed in the garden, but at night we kept them here. The sharp pebbles dug into my bare feet. I was light-headed; I'd gotten up too fast. As I approached, Pomme put down her shovel. A few chickens fussed somewhere in their coop, but the wheelbarrow was full of mangled carcasses.

"What got them?" I asked. It didn't look like coyotes or bears. These chickens were just mauled and then dropped. I thought I saw Sadie and Pomme share a glance.

"What?" I asked. I wanted to sit down.

"Was Ulla out when you got home last night?" Pomme asked.

I nodded. Pomme and Sadie were already in bed, their door closed tight, even though it was only eight o'clock.

"Well, you should've brought her in."

"Where is she?" I asked. "Is she okay?"

Pomme sniffed. I stared at Sadie, but she wouldn't meet my eye.

"It's okay now," she said. "We'll get new ones."

"But—"

Pomme turned and lifted another carcass into the wheelbarrow. I'd never had to look out for Ulla. It wasn't fair. Pomme should've brought her in herself. But the thought of her burying her dog here in the yard made my skin tingle with sweat.

"I put her in my truck," said Pomme, finally.

"Oh."

The pickup bed was empty. I frowned. I crossed around to the driver's door and peered in. She was on the seat. I put my hand on the window. It's true I didn't like the dog but I didn't want her dead. Then she twitched.

"Hey," I said.

The dog leapt up and threw her face against the glass. I stumbled back as she barked. I threw the door open. She jumped out and barked at me until Pomme gripped her collar and tossed her back in the cab. Closer, I saw feathers on the seat and blood on her fur. I gaped at Pomme but she just shrugged.

"They're animals, Cassiopeia."

"Are you kidding me?" I laughed and looked to Sadie but she wouldn't meet my eyes.

I reddened as I watched Pomme trundle down toward the garden. She'd dug a hole next to the compost heap. I peered into the truck.

"Stupid dog," I said through the glass. Ulla chewed frantically at her back. She was repenting.

I grabbed some gumboots and stepped into the coop, still light-headed. All I wanted to do was crawl back into bed. I undid the latch for the door we used to collect eggs. The hens were nervous in the corner but they looked all right.

"It's okay, girls," I said.

They scattered around me. I pulled some feed out and tossed it into their yard. One by one they ventured out. We'd lost seven altogether. There were five left. As I rummaged around for eggs, the warm smell of them wafted up and my stomach churned. I swallowed. The smell had never grossed me out; we'd had chickens for as long as I could remember. But the henhouse was suddenly stifling and thick. I tried to ignore it, checking all the nests. No one had laid this morning. It could be ages before they were regular again if they were all traumatized. Nausea waved over me and I puked onto a pile of wood shavings, then again. I wiped my mouth. I didn't feel better like I had yesterday. I felt awful. I had to lie down.

Outside, I fumbled the gate latch and threw up on my boots.

"Sweetheart."

Sadie reached out to touch my forehead and I swiped at her. I didn't want her to get involved.

◆

That afternoon I wandered over to Kendall's house, but she wasn't there. Auntie Trish was unpacking groceries in the kitchen. She was only a few years older than Sadie, but she looked aged. She'd lived differently, I guess, and it showed in her face. Sadie was more easygoing than Trish. She didn't take too much on. Sometimes that annoyed me; I couldn't always rely on her to notice things, or be on time if I needed her. But Auntie Trish had her own problems and the way she took life on didn't help her case.

Kendall and Lucas's dad, Russ, was an electrician in Vancouver and an alcoholic. He went on a lot of benders, bad enough that the kids couldn't live with him even though I'm sure they wished they could a lot of the time. They saw him once or twice a year for a weekend.

Trish left Russ when Kendall was six, just after Lucas was born. She moved back to the island, took over the old family cabin and hired someone to fix up the windows and insulate the main room. Piece by piece the place became livable in the winter. When she added an extension, she tried to make it look modern and clean, but it was a strange effect. The old part of the cabin was rustic and cozy, but when you crossed into the second portion of the house, the back rec room and the master bedroom, it was like you were walking into a lotto house. I preferred the cabin. I was born in one of the bedrooms. There was a faded yellow star on the plywood floor where my mother had given birth to me. She was twenty years old, and a midwife and a couple of friends looked on.

My grandparents raised their two daughters in town on Vancouver Island but kept the cabin for summers and went there often. Sadie always thought they would have been real islanders if there'd been much community but there were only hermits here until Sadie was a teenager. When Sadie was eighteen Grandpa died in a logging accident and Granny died a year later of heart failure.

I think it was hard for Sadie when Granny died. She got pregnant the same month. She'd always told me she didn't know who my dad was. It was the early eighties, she'd explain, as if that was supposed to excuse it all for me. I'd never figured the eighties were that wild of a time, but what did I know. If she ever had an idea of who he was, she never let on. Whoever he was, he was obviously long gone.

That afternoon, I sat at Aunt Trish's kitchen table and watched her unpack the food as I waited for Kendall. Trish seemed grumpy as usual.

"She took Lucas to the coffee shop for donuts," she said, then shook her head like that was a stupid thing to do. "If only she cared about her own life half as much as she liked her little brother."

"It's nice," I offered, but Trish just snorted.

"She's going to end up like her father if she keeps this up," she said. "Not like you. You've got a good head on your shoulders."

I put my head down. Not such a good head. I thought about my day planner stashed under the bed. If only she knew. Kendall might be wild sometimes but I was now permanently stained.

"I think she's doing okay," I said finally, pushing aside the memory of Martin spitting his own cum out on the steps of Kendall's condemned hangout. I wondered if there was a way to tell Trish how delicately balanced it all looked from my perspective, how wrong it could all go. They just had to make it to Kendall's eighteenth birthday in October.

Trish set a cup of tea in front of me and sat down. All the groceries put away and Auntie Trish done complaining about her daughter, we didn't have much to say to each other. We had family dinners from time to time, but even Trish and Sadie didn't get together often. It was like they were from completely different corners of the earth and had no context for each other.

Eventually, I got up and told her I had to be going.

"Do you need a ride somewhere?" she asked. "Aren't you going to work soon?"

I did have to work, and it was a fair distance to walk, but my shift didn't start for another two hours and I didn't want to be early. Maybe if I started out toward the village I would run into Kendall and Lucas. I told Aunt Trish I'd be fine and waved goodbye.

Out on the road, it started to drizzle. I cursed as I realized I'd worn flip-flops. You weren't supposed to wear flip-flops at the Village Grocery in case a stock boy dropped something on your toes or you had to run after somebody who forgot their credit card.

Fifteen minutes into my walk I hadn't spotted my cousins and it was still raining. A truck appeared in the distance and I decided to try hitching. I squinted, trying to gauge if I knew the person just like Kendall had taught me. When the truck was close enough that I could tell the driver wasn't my old math teacher or my boss, and also not an obvious serial killer, I stuck my thumb out.

The truck slowed as it passed but didn't stop. A man about Sadie's age leaned over and squinted at me. A few yards down the road he finally inched to a halt. I walked over. It was a dusty red truck. Inside, the floor was littered with lottery tickets and paper cups, and the cracks of the seat were filled with sand. It smelled like diesel and hot coffee, which was nice in a strange way.

I climbed in and nodded to the man, trying to look confident. He was good-looking—not obviously, but once you looked close enough. He was younger than he first appeared, younger than his age even.

"I don't usually pick up hitchhikers," he said.

"Thanks." I shoved my hands in my sweater pockets.

"Where are you going?"

I told him I was going to the village and he nodded. The radio was soft, on talk radio, and the windshield wipers fanned across the glass once in a while. It was warm in the truck. The man took a sip of coffee and put the cup back in the holder.

"You look familiar," he said without taking his eyes off the road.

I shrugged. I told him I'd lived here my whole life and he glanced at me.

"Are your parents from around here?"

"My mum is," I said. "Sadie Mitchell."

"Sadie," he said, searching his memory. "Sadie."

"I've never seen you before," I said.

"I lived here about ten years ago. I just came back to help an old friend out with his farm by Sung Spit."

"I didn't know anyone lived out there."

"Sure they do."

"The beach houses are abandoned now," I said, though I wasn't sure why. Maybe if he'd been away for so long he wouldn't have noticed. He glanced at me and said the farm where he was staying was on the point just after the Spit, then was quiet for a while.

"I thought one or two of the houses still had tenants in there."

I shook my head and looked out the window. For some reason I wanted to tell him about the cabins, Kendall's and mine. Maybe he'd heard us there. Sound travelled far on water. Kendall had probably been there without me since we'd discovered them. Maybe she'd even found a way to rig up a stereo and invited other people in. I thought about Kendall taking Martin into her seventies house with its shag carpet and damp walls and decided I wouldn't want to see this man walking out of that house.

We turned left at the only traffic lights on the island. The village, as it was called, was the grocery store, a café, a movie rental place, some kitschy hippy stores that were only open in the tourist months and a cold beer and wine. There was a pub, small restaurant and another grocery store on the other side of the island by the marina but that was about it. Somewhere in the hard-to-reach coves there were resorts and a place for high-end dining but they weren't for locals. You could almost completely forget they were there. Sadie cleaned some of the rooms once in a while if they were short-staffed, but mostly the places were run completely by outsiders who rarely ventured into town.

"Thanks for the ride," I said as we pulled into the parking lot. I was an hour early for my shift, but I could kill time somehow.

"I'm Robert, by the way," he said and held out his hand.

"Cassiopeia," I said.

He laughed and squeezed my hand. I blushed. His hands were calloused and warm. I couldn't think of the last time I'd shaken a man's hand. I asked him why he was laughing.

"Quite the name."

"It makes sense if you know my mom." I shrugged. "My cousin calls me Cassie."

He shook his head. "Doesn't suit you."

"No," I agreed. "Well, see you around."

I ducked out of the truck and into Village Grocery. I sat in the break room for an hour in my staff shirt and flip-flops reading discarded magazines until my shift started.

A few nights later, Kendall and I went to a movie in town. We planned to meet on the five o'clock ferry and walk to the theatre from the terminal. I usually went into town five days a week for school, and I was beginning to feel cooped up on the island. There were only so many variables to a day, and it made anyone but the hermits a bit restless.

I stood in my bedroom in front of the mirror getting ready. I'd brushed my hair until it was flat and shiny and put on a dress. My favourite shorts from last summer were too tight now; I couldn't tell if it was because I'd grown or because I was bloated all the time. I stood perfectly still in front of my reflection and stared at my face. The freckles on my nose were starting to show, just like they always did once the sun came out. Without taking my eyes off my face, I gathered the hem of my dress in my fingers and I pulled the fabric up to my waist. Then, finally, I let my eyes drop to my abdomen. I turned sideways, carefully, trying to make my eyes focus on the gently swollen shape my body was taking on. I dropped the dress.

Almost two months had passed since Elliot and I had sex the last time. A week and a half later I started worrying, and a few days later we broke up in the incommunicative way of teenagers. I didn't tell him I was terrified. Instead I acted like I was pissed off. Then, because it was too much to deal with, I just stopped talking to him. What was he going to do anyway? I was too embarrassed. We'd both made a mistake, but it was *my* body that had turned on me. It was suddenly doing things I couldn't control. I was the burden. Whenever I thought about it, I was overwhelmed with embarrassment.

I gathered my sandals and bag. Sadie wasn't home, so I slipped into her bedroom where it was dark, the curtains drawn to keep it cool. I'd been steering clear of her and Pomme since the chicken incident but Sadie kept her pot in an old, frayed purse next to her shoes and I wanted it.

I opened the closet, listening out for Pomme, and helped myself to a small bud. Occasionally, she'd dole out little bits if I asked, but made me promise not to tell Trish. It was hard to find someone on the island who would sell to us since Kendall had started getting in shit, but she could get some with a glance at Alternative. It all seemed backwards; if they just shared with us we'd be better off. The shake in town was nearly chemical. I slipped back into my room just as Sadie came through the front door.

◈

I found Kendall slouched behind the electrical box by the ferry waiting room and sat next to her. The ferry docked as the water churned and the foot passengers milled around behind the safety rope.

"I got some," I said.

She grinned but she looked kind of down.

"Do you have any rollies?"

"No, don't you?"

I shook my head.

She chewed her lip. Something was bothering her. Half the people on the ferry probably had rollies in their pockets but we didn't want to ask them. We'd have to wait until we were on the other side, in town. We could take a detour down Main Street. There'd be someone outside the skate shop that sold blown-glass pipes who could help us out. We used to have one of those pipes but we lost it on the beach one night.

"What's wrong?" I asked as we boarded the boat.

"My mum's getting on my back," she said. "She thinks I should go back to summer school."

I didn't say anything. I would have been relieved to see Kendall back in school, too, but I knew she wouldn't go. We went upstairs, to the little passenger area. There was a small outdoor deck and enough seats for everyone. In the middle of the boat was an empty cafeteria with its metal window guard rolled down. No one had ever, ever seen it open. Instead, it had been turned into a sort of bulletin board. Anyone with sticky tape could post something. The thing was covered in posters and fliers. Sometimes I read them. Some of them were for hippy dance parties at the Hall, but usually off-the-track tourists put hand-written notes up there. They were always looking to rent a cabin on the beach for the summer or hoping to find some part-time work for a month or two. No one ever called those people as far as I could tell, and eventually they would move on.

I went to the washroom and when I came out Kendall wasn't at her seat. I wandered around, not bothering to say hi to every second person. Finally I spotted her outside on the lifejacket trunk with a guy in his twenties. They passed a joint back and forth. Man, she was quick. I stood inside and pretended not to watch them. She looked so confident, the wind whipping her hair, her sunglasses pulled down. She looked different with strangers than she did with us. She looked happier.

When the boat churned into the dock, she found me reading the message board. She grinned and flashed me a few joints and rollies.

The theatre was a fifteen-minute walk from the terminal. The movie didn't start until seven fifteen so we had plenty of time to smoke pot, buy some penny candy and find a good seat. Everyone went to the backwoods between the theatre and the hardware store to smoke before the movie, but you had to pick your place carefully. We were island kids, so we were always at the bottom of the pecking order. It didn't matter how tough you were—if you were from the island you were considered a hippy and soft. Kendall had made her way into some of the tougher crowds because of Alternative, but she still couldn't waltz into any backwoods and expect to run the place. Island kids had to smoke at the edge of the lot, by the back of the theatre, which was the worst because that was the first place anyone ever got busted.

When we got there a group of twelve-year-olds goofed off by the stumps. I recognized some of them from school and the island, but most of them were townies. They were already high and making too much noise. Kendall rolled her eyes.

I'd always liked smoking pot, but I had liked it more in the last couple of months because it settled my stomach. I'd found myself wanting to smoke it alone in the evenings after Sadie and Pomme went to bed, or before dinner so I could show up with a proper appetite. I couldn't, obviously, because I rarely had any but maybe I could convince Kendall to give me one of the ferry guy's joints if we didn't smoke them all tonight. I rolled because I was better at it. My fingers were slimmer than hers and I was quicker.

"Where's your lighter?" I asked.

She smacked her head. "That guy has it."

I groaned. We couldn't just wander into the gas station and buy a lighter. The only place was a corner store run by an old Chinese guy where you could get just about anything, even smokes once in a while, but that was far across town.

"You have to try," she said.

"Can't we just ask the tweens?"

"They'll mooch."

I sighed. Usually, I would give up right then. I hated being turned down; it was humiliating. But I wanted that pot. Across from the theatre was a plaza with a chain grocery and drugstore.

"Okay," I said, walking away. "But you can't come."

I didn't look back as I darted across the main road and paused on the meridian to let cars pass. I pulled my legs through a hedge of wild roses and ignored the stinging scratches.

Inside, the air conditioning was almost frigid. I crossed my arms over my chest. My breasts had been sore for a while now, the way they were just before I got my period, but now they were starting to hurt less. Or maybe I was just getting used to it. I walked down the aisles, pretending to shop. The lighters were up at the customer service counter with the smokes and the lotto tickets. I couldn't just roll up and buy a single lighter; they'd never go for it. I wandered over to the candy isle and picked up a pack of gummy worms. Kendall would want chips but they only had big bags and I didn't want to spend that much money.

I walked past the makeup counters and into the pharmacy section. It was quiet. It was Friday evening; everyone was out having a barbeque or swimming. I suddenly wished I was at home, or at the beach with Sadie like we used to do in the evening after she finished work. The sun would be a gold orange down there right now and the smell of beach fire and dry pine needles would be in the air. I wanted to run into the water and stay there, floating on my back or practising summersaults underwater until it was dark, just like when I was kid. Tears came to my eyes and I wiped them away. What was wrong with me?

I stopped in front of the feminine products isle. There were two types of pregnancy tests. One was three dollars cheaper than the other one. Before I could stop myself, I snatched it, my heart beating. I passed a cashier, standing there, waiting for the store to close. The evening sun came in through the front windows. It looked incredible outside, better than it really was.

I placed my gummy worms and pregnancy test on top of the lotto display counter. My face was blazing. It took a minute for the middle-aged woman to notice me, but when she saw what I was buying she stared for a minute, then grabbed it and scanned it through quickly.

"And a lighter," I said. "A pink one."

She nodded and took one from the display case behind her. She looked worn out. She was probably a smoker. Her crimped hair was dyed black. She handed me the plastic bag and I passed her a crumpled twenty. As I walked out the automatic doors, I heard her call to me.

"Good luck," she said.

To my surprise, I found Kendall alone in the movie theatre parking lot where I'd left her. The line for the ticket booth was three people out the door; we didn't have much time. It was the only theatre in town and had a single screen so if there was a half-decent movie the place could easily fill up.

Around back, a big group had congregated in the woods. We'd be quick and discreet; we weren't fooling around. Get stoned, get in line, get a decent seat. I turned my back to the crowd of stoners behind us and pretended not to listen to them as I lit the joint. I had just taken my first hit when Kendall grabbed my arm and squeezed.

"What *the fuck*," she said and squeezed harder.

The next thing I knew she was storming into the crowd of people. I watched in horror as she pushed through the townies like she owned the place. But then, behind the crowd, I saw what she saw: her little brother in a cloud of smoke, laughing like a maniac.

He squealed that awful prepubescent squeal of a twelve-year-old as she dragged him away from his friends. Some of the townies hooted and laughed. Everyone watched on. It was better than any movie that'd be playing here tonight.

"*Lucas*," she cried when they'd reached me.

She had a death grip on his upper arm. I'd never seen Kendall care so much about anything. I watched in amazement as she tried to calm herself enough to speak. Lucas was trying to laugh and look tough, but it wasn't working. Soon the crowd of townies forgot about us and turned away.

Lucas twisted free.

"What's your problem?"

"You're in so much shit," she said.

Lucas's voice raised several octaves as he pointed out that Kendall smoked pot all the time.

"*You're twelve*," she said.

"You've been doing way worse since you were thirteen!" he cried.

It was true; there was no denying that. I slipped the half-burned joint back into my bag and sighed. The movie line was getting longer and I had to pee. Kendall grabbed Lucas's arm again. He flinched. She had a killer grip, I knew from experience. I felt for the kid, but I was surprised to see him here, too. I guess I hadn't seen much of him in the last couple of months, but he'd changed so quickly. His bone structure was different. He'd lost some of his baby fat and there was a faint suggestion of a moustache above his lip. How had it happened? Lucas was a teenager.

"It's not a big deal," he said and started to walk away, not back toward the woods but to the road. He was freaked out. I couldn't help it; I burst out laughing. Kendall frowned at me.

"He's totally high," I said. "You're tripping him out."

We watched him shuffle down the sidewalk alone. He was a classic tweaker in that moment. Kendall's laughter spilled out and soon we were hysterical. When we finally calmed down, I could tell Kendall felt better. It was like nothing had ever happened. I don't know how she did it, but I was relieved to see her back to her old self.

When she reached into my bag for the candy I held my breath. If she noticed the pregnancy test, she didn't say so.

After the movie, we had to sprint for the last ferry. We ripped through the wild roses, through the parking lots, around the cluster of totem poles in a small park and over Main Street. Finally, gasping, we ran straight onto the ferry ramp just as the ferry guy flashed the *all clear* signal. Missing the last boat was nothing to joke about. You were in absolute shit if you did. We'd thought about fixing up an old row boat for such emergencies, but our moms had caught wind of the plan and told us no way in hell were we making that crossing at ten thirty in the dark. So we ran like our lives depended on it.

We sprinted onto the car deck, winded. I folded over. I was so dizzy I thought I might pass out. I wanted to sit down but there was nowhere close. My forehead burned and I felt like I was going to puke. I rushed to the edge of the boat but it didn't come. I leaned my head against the cool iron of the stern and let the nausea pass. When I looked up Kendall just laughed and told me I must be out of shape.

Upstairs, Kendall flopped onto the back row of seats and I went to the washroom. I splashed my face over the tiny sink, then went into one of the two stalls. It was almost completely dark in the stalls. It had been that way for as long as I could remember. There must have been light at one time, but it had long since burned out and now you just had to pee in the dim, narrow stall. I was alone, so I pulled out the plastic bag from the drugstore and opened the box. I didn't want to do this here, but I couldn't do it at home or someone would find it. I unfolded the instructions on my lap and squinted at the diagrams. I looked down at the plastic stick. How complicated could it be? It didn't even matter; I was almost positive I was pregnant. I crumpled the instructions up and shoved them in the metal bin for dirty pads and took the cap off the stick. I just had to pee on it, I knew that much.

I held the stick out and accidentally peed on my hand. I cursed. I couldn't see much in the dark so after a few minutes I stuck my head out of the stall to make sure I was alone, then darted out. I held the test over the sink and squinted at it. Both the windows had little pink pluses. My heart pounded. My heart pounding surprised me more than the test itself. Wasn't I expecting it?

Behind me, the door swung open and I looked up in the mirror just in time to see a girl from my school. I shoved the test in the garbage can, but it was too late. She'd seen. She stood in the doorway and stared at me with a smugness that made me wish I could punch her out. Tears welled up but I pushed them down as I grabbed my bag and darted out the door. I prayed that the test was covered by paper towel, but it didn't matter. It was bad enough to be caught taking a pregnancy test. The outcome was almost irrelevant.

I was shaking as I found Kendall slouched in her seat and told her to get up.

"Come with me," I hissed.

She jumped up and followed me to the outer deck where it was dark and private. I jumped onto the lifejacket trunk and buried my face.

"What?" she asked, but I could only shake my head.

My face burned. What was that girl doing on our boat? She wasn't an islander. She was a grade younger than me. I didn't know much about her, but she was pretty in that sort of quiet, smart kind of way. She had definitely never taken a pregnancy test before, especially in a dingy ferry stall. I groaned.

"What?" Kendall asked again and laughed.

I couldn't tell her, not like this. I wanted her to know, I wanted her to help me but I wasn't ready for it to be real like that. I forced myself to laugh and fake a shrug. She rolled her eyes.

"You're so weird," she said.

Down on the main deck, as we zigzagged through idling cars while the boat docked, it suddenly made sense. There, at the front of the bow with a few other walk-ons, were Elliot and the bathroom girl. I stopped as soon as I saw them, but it was too late. She caught my eye and I saw her reach for Elliot's hand and squeeze it. He turned and looked at me. She'd told him what she'd seen in the bathroom and now she was pointing out the stupid slut she'd walked in on. I wanted to turn around and hide until all the cars were off, but it was too late. He'd spotted me. I could tell by the surprise on his face that it hadn't occurred to him that the slut was me. The girl laughed and leaned into him. She was still holding his hand; they were holding hands. His eyes stayed on mine, expressionless. Then he turned slowly, back to the girl, and shrugged.

I called in sick to work the next day. Sadie didn't know my schedule so didn't think anything of it as she kissed me goodbye at the breakfast table and left to clean houses. I sat with a soggy bowl of cereal in front of me. The clock ticked on the wall until I finally got up and went outside. We had an old bathtub on the porch with a firepit underneath and a garden hose rigged to the side. Sadie had found it at the back of the recycling depot years ago and paid a neighbour to hoist it into the bed of his pickup. I think it was her favourite thing in the world besides the garden. I often found her, limbs draped over the side in the steaming water at dusk. She must have been busy or distracted with Pomme lately because it was full of wood bugs and bits of leaves.

After I wiped it out, I started the fire and blasted the hose. It would heat up quickly especially in the sun. I eased in, goosebumps rippling down my legs. The fire crackled underneath me and the sun came in warm off the cedar planks of the porch.

I stretched my legs out and looked down at my naked body. I felt big today, even though I didn't look any different. The embarrassment of last night's ferry ride was wearing off, and now I was left with a dull ache that wouldn't go away. Elliot had a new girlfriend. I was alone. I might have come around and asked him for help, but now I couldn't. He'd clearly moved on from the situation, whereas I had hardly begun to deal with it.

I looked down again at my belly. I just wanted it gone. I wanted to have a good summer and go back to school in the fall. I wanted to smoke pot and pass a two-litre cider bottle back and forth with Kendall in the movie theatre. I didn't want to have a serious conversation with my mom, or get a ride down to Victoria for an abortion, which is where girls at school said you had to go. I just wanted to be a normal sixteen-year-old again. I gripped the side of the tub and thought about punching myself in the stomach. Maybe that would work. But I couldn't make my fist do it. Please, I thought, let me get my period. Just like that. I promise I'll be better. I'll be careful. I didn't even want to have sex ever again.

I cried in the tub for a long time, angry at first, then pathetic. Eventually I got out and poured a bucket of water on the fire. I gave myself a deadline: by the end of the week I had to tell someone. I called Kendall but no one picked up.

That afternoon, I walked. I didn't know where I was going, to Sung Spit, or maybe into town. I just had to move. I stood at the intersection in the village. Something would have to happen if I just kept moving. But I had blisters and was starving from not eating all day I was heading to the grocery store when I remembered that I'd called in sick.

"Shit," I muttered and darted through the lights.

Where could I go? I couldn't make it to Sung Spit. I was shaky from hunger and light-headed. If I walked to the cabins now I might never make it back alive. I had ten dollars in my pocket. I could take the boat over to town and wander around there for a while. I would have enough money for a slice of pizza or something from the vending machine in the waiting room on the other side. It seemed like a pretty pathetic way to spend an afternoon, but I had nothing else to do.

I cut down the road that turned into the ferry lineup. The last few cars were easing onto the ramp. I sighed I would never make it. I couldn't run right now if my life depended on it and I didn't want to wait forty minutes until it came back. I wandered back up to the intersection in the village and risked running into my manager or whoever got called in to cover my shift.

I went into the café and ordered some mint tea and a bagel, the two cheapest things on the blackboard. As I waited at the end of the counter, I noticed Robert on the pay phone in the back corner. I gave him a small wave and he smiled back. I was stirring honey into my tea when he wandered over.

"Cassiopeia."

"Hi," I said.

We stepped out under the awning of the plaza. The sky was dark and humid with clouds. A summer storm was brewing. Within seconds, a curtain of raindrops pounded the parking lot in front of us.

"You want a ride somewhere?" he asked.

"Where are you going?" I asked.

"I just dropped someone off at the ferry. I was heading back to the farm, but I don't mind dropping you at home or wherever you need to go. Hell of a walk in the rain."

I stared out at the parking lot. Thunder sounded somewhere in the distance. These summer storms were rare. You got one, maybe two a year. There was nothing quite like them, how the air was warm and charged, dangerous and cozy all at once. It sounded crazy, but this was the best swimming weather. Kendall and I used to race to the beach when it rained like this. The ocean became bathwater and there was something satisfying about being poured on when you were already wet.

"I'm meeting my cousin on the beach before the Spit," I lied.

Robert hesitated, then agreed to drop me off before his farm. I climbed into the truck. It was cleaner inside now. There was still a lot of gravel and pine needles on the seat, but the coffee cups and lotto tickets were gone. Maybe it had something to do with the guest he'd just dropped off at the ferry.

"Strange place to hang out," he said, turning left at the lights.

I shrugged and took a bite of my bagel. I told him it wasn't like there was anything better to do. That was the first time I realized it was true.

Kendall wasn't in her seventies cabin, or any of them. The rain stopped, but the electric charge was still rampant. Lightning flashed on the horizon. I had that strange feeling like something was happening, out there in the world, but I was stuck here without a soul around, miles from anything, bored to death. I sat on a damp log and finished my tea. My stomach was a hard lump. I felt awful.

Where was Kendall? Sometimes she disappeared for days without notice. She'd go to town and stay with a friend, or only come home at night to appease Trish, then disappear in the morning, just often enough that Trish couldn't get mad. I thought it might be different this summer; I thought she might bring me with her. I was going to go insane if I didn't have something to do other than walk around and work at the grocery store. For a moment, I even missed Elliot.

Behind me, through the trees and down the path, I heard voices. Men. I jumped up and hid behind one of the boarded-up houses. They came down the path and after a few seconds I realized they were cops. They milled around for a few minutes, talking, then one of them pointed down the beach and the others dispersed. I recognized the one giving orders; he'd busted Kendall and me with smuggled homemade wine a few years ago. Now he stood in the doorway of Kendall's cabin but didn't go in.

As they wandered around, I strained to listen. Someone needed to call the developer down here, someone said, to properly board the place up. Trespassing, someone else muttered. I rolled my eyes. Island cops didn't have anything better to do than take a full squad field trip.

I sighed as they trudged back up to the road. When I was sure they were gone, I wandered back to the cabins. Police tape crisscrossed Kendall's front door. It would only tempt her. I reached out and gripped the tape. A chill went through me like I was being watched. I tore it down and fled.

I didn't know where else to go, so I walked down the beach until I found the grassy orchard that jutted out over the ocean and climbed the sandy bank. There was an old barbed wire fence; my hair got caught but I pulled myself through and stood in the long grass. It was beautiful here. The long meadow was full of knobby dwarf apple trees and the land sloped up to an old house with a tarped roof. I heard a rooster in the distance, and pigs. Beyond that there was a field full of overgrown canola, yellow and buttery.

I remembered this farm now. I'd never been here, but I remembered going to the Sunday morning market with Sadie when I was a kid. There was an old man, Arthur I think his name was, with the best food. It was his farm. As I made my way through the long, itchy grass to the house I wondered if he was still around.

Robert sat alone on the porch with reading glasses and a cup of coffee. I waved and he stood up, confused at first, then amused. I stopped on the rickety steps to the porch and shielded my eyes from the sun, strangely bright behind the loosening clouds.

"Hi," I said.

"Your cousin wasn't there?"

"No." I looked down at my dirty flip-flops. "I guess I was too late."

"You want a cup of tea or something?" He dropped his newspaper on his chair.

I shrugged and nodded. The wind picked up and rustled through a big willow in the driveway. Robert went inside for a while and came out with a mug. I sat down next to him and we didn't say anything for a while.

"This is Arthur's farm, right?" I asked.

Robert looked surprised. "You know him?"

I shook my head. "Not really. It's a small town."

"Right," he said. "It's his but not for long. He's in a nursing home now. I came to help care for the animals while his assets get sorted out."

I asked him if he used to live here on the farm, ten years ago like he'd told me when I first met him. He nodded.

"I worked for Arthur when he had a bar in Whistler a long time ago. I came up here one summer in my twenties and ran into him. He always needed help around the place in the summer so I used to come up whenever I was out of a job."

I didn't say anything for a long time. I imagined him as a young man. He probably had a big beard and a dirty backpack, just like old photos I'd seen of transients in the seventies. Maybe he came and went over the years before he stayed ten years ago.

"Did you know my mom?" I asked. "Sadie?"

He squinted out at the willow. "Rings a bell. Maybe if I saw her face."

I sighed. I was so tired I could barely keep my eyes open.

"Is it just you here?" I asked.

He nodded.

"Who were you dropping off at the ferry?" I asked, knowing it was none of my business.

"A friend of mine."

"A woman?" I asked.

"Uh," he said. "Yes, a woman."

I nodded. I was tired right down to my bones.

"Do you mind if I take a nap on your couch?" I asked. "Just for a little while."

By the time I was wrapped in an old knitted throw on the couch I was fast asleep.

I tried calling Kendall all throughout the next day, but no one picked up. Finally on my fourth try, in the late afternoon, Lucas answered.

"She and my mom went into town," he said. "They're at the doctor's."

"Why?" I asked.

"Someone punched Kendall," he said.

I frowned. "Who? What happened?"

"I don't know. Something happened the other night after the movie. I was at my friend's. They'll be back on the four thirty."

I hung up. It didn't make any sense. I went down to the garden and found Sadie head down in the weeds. I told her I needed a ride to Kendall's. She sighed and pulled her gloves off.

"Can't you walk?" she asked.

My voice cracked as I told her something had happened to Kendall. But when she didn't seem too concerned, I banged through the flimsy chicken wire gate and took off up the driveway alone.

❖

When their car pulled up to the house, I was sitting on the porch waiting. Lucas was inside playing video games. Kendall got out first and slammed the car door. Her right eye was red and swollen. She trudged past, giving me the slightest glance, then slammed the house door, too.

"Don't you start that," Trish called after her, but there was some doubt in her voice.

She held the door for me without saying anything. I nodded at her, tentative, unsure how friendly I should be. I was forever on Kendall's side, willing to give anyone the cold shoulder for her sake, but Auntie Trish looked more exhausted than anything so I let my face soften.

I found Kendall in her room. What a strange room it was. It was almost devoid of personal touches. All traces of childhood had been disposed of, unlike my room with its patchwork quilt and flowery curtains. Kendall's room was simple: an old brown duvet on the bed, a closet and a dresser. The only sign of a teenager was a mound of dirty clothes on the floor and a stack of CDs on a chair. Her old bedside table with stickers was long gone. She'd painted her dresser a deep purple, almost black.

She sat on the floor, looking far away. Her eye looked awful, tender. My own eye twinged in sympathy. I bent down and hugged her around the arms. She didn't give any response so I squeezed her tighter, then let go and stared at her.

"What happened?" I finally asked.

"Some freak punched me in the eye, that's what happened."

"When? Who?"

She sighed, exasperated, like she was sick of talking about it. But it was *me*. I would listen to her. I gripped her hand and she gave me the tiniest squeeze back. I couldn't imagine what kind of trouble she could have found on a Monday night on the island. All I'd done was go home, brush my teeth and fall into bed. How did she do it?

"I went to the gas station to see if I could buy smokes," she said.

"Martin punched you?" I said, incredulous, but she shook her head.

"No, one of his friends. We went down to the cabins. They had some coke."

"What did you *do*?" I asked before I could stop myself.

Kendall dropped my hand and I instantly regretted it. She clenched her fist.

"*Nothing*," she said. "You think someone deserves to be punched, like I was asking for it?"

"No," I said. But I wasn't sure. "I'm sorry."

She shook her head. "No one will listen to me. I made my mom call the police this morning. Everyone just keeps asking me what I was doing down there in the middle of the night with those guys, like it's all my fault."

I shook my head. This place seemed more and more messed up. I looked carefully at her eye again, and then told her how I went down to the beach yesterday to look for her and saw the cops. She sat up straighter.

"What were they doing?"

"Looking around," I said. "It sounded like they were going to board it all up."

"All those pigs care about is trespassing."

She flopped back on her bed.

"Trish is talking about sending Lucas to boarding school in Victoria," she said, "so he doesn't turn out like me."

I glanced down at my hands. I wanted to distract her. She didn't have to be miserable alone. I was in shit, too, and frankly, I needed her help. I took a deep breath.

"I told her about him smoking pot."

I looked at her, shocked.

"I'm just trying to look out for him and she blamed *me*. But boarding school. Don't you know how fucked up those places are?"

I didn't. But I could imagine. No doubt Trish had them both

on lockdown. Kendall couldn't live like that. I asked if she wanted to stay at our house for a while but she shook her head.

"What are you going to do?" I asked.

"I don't know."

"Kendall," I said. "I have to tell you something."

"What?" she said, but didn't sit up.

"I'm kind of pregnant."

She rolled her head toward me.

"Are you going to have an abortion?" she asked.

"Yeah."

She didn't speak for a long time. At first I wondered if she was high; she was barely there. It was like she'd hardly heard me. But I looked closer and realized she was furious. Her bruised eye twitched. This wasn't her standard high-strung angst; it was hatred.

A couple nights later, Sadie and Trish sat on our porch in the late sun. I'd caught a ride home from work with a girl from the meat department and they hushed when they saw me come down the driveway. They were conspiring about something; I knew that look when I saw it.

"Cassiopeia," Sadie said as I clunked up the porch steps.

"What?" I was still mad at both of them for not worrying more about Kendall. What kind of mothers were they? What kind of women?

Sadie squinted at me. "How was work?"

"Fine." I slid the screen door open.

"Come back for a second," she called.

I clunked back out. I'd been given a warning at work about the flip-flops. No matter how hard I tried, I couldn't remember not to wear them. The only shoes I had that fit me besides my worn-out gym shoes were my hiking boots, so I'd been stomping around in them all day. I stepped extra hard around my manager to make sure she hadn't overlooked my obedience.

"What?" I sat on the arm of an Adirondack.

"Who's this man you've been driving around with?" she asked.

I frowned. "No one."

"Someone told me they saw you."

I scoffed. She'd hardly paid attention to me in the last few months since Pomme moved in, and now she was suddenly taking an interest? She didn't care if I spent the night at Elliot's or if I showed up after dark without calling, but now she'd decided to care about me getting a ride from someone? I asked her how else I was supposed to get around when she wouldn't drive me anywhere and had raised me in the utter boonies

"Do you think it's a good idea?" she asked. "Getting rides from strangers?"

"You don't really care," I said and stood up.

"Look what's happening to your cousin," said Trish. "You want to end up like her?"

"Screw you," I said.

Trish blinked and Sadie just stared at me. I couldn't believe they were unabashedly blaming her for being attacked. I didn't care what she did; she didn't deserve to be punched in the face by a man. I took a deep breath, prepared for a weak attempt to discipline me, but nothing came. Finally, Trish looked at me.

"Have you heard from her?" Her voice was quieter now. She almost sounded afraid.

"What do you mean?" I sat down in the chair. My stomach churned. "Where is she?"

"Oh, she took off somewhere," Auntie Trish said, trying to sound nonchalant. But there was doubt in her voice. She waved her hand. "She probably went down to Vancouver to see her deadbeat dad."

"She's not in town?" I asked.

"Well, someone said they saw her at the bus depot last night."

"She wouldn't just leave," I cried, suddenly feeling sick. How could she have left without telling me?

"I had the police out looking for her, wasting taxpayers' dollars." I stared at Aunt Trish.

"What if she's in trouble?" I asked, my chin trembling. I stood up. I wanted to kick them. They were pathetic, sitting there.

"She thinks she can handle herself," said Trish. She wouldn't meet my eye. She was either terrified or pissed off; that was the strange thing about Trish, the two were almost inseparable.

"That man beat her up and you didn't do anything," I cried, but I was thinking about myself, of how she could leave me now.

"Cassiopeia," said Sadie, but I slammed the screen door and rushed for my bedroom.

The next morning, the police knocked on our door. Sadie was late for work but lingered as they stepped in and asked me a few questions about Kendall. I recognized them from the beach the other afternoon. The guy giving orders, Sergeant Nygren, leaned over with his knuckles pressed into the kitchen table and squinted at me. He looked dead serious and was brisk in his questioning. He was trying to make me feel like I'd burned down an orphanage or backed over all the puppies. I raised my chin just slightly and ignored the lump in my throat as I told him just about everything I was willing to confess about Kendall in a steady, curt voice.

"Do you know where your cousin is?" he asked.

"No," I said.

He nodded like he thought I was full of shit and was going to figure out just how to make me confess. I didn't appreciate him. I wanted my cousin back; I wanted her safe more than anyone else. I wondered if he remembered Kendall and me from years ago when he made us pour our wine into the ditch and called our mothers in the middle of night. Kendall had been grounded for weeks. It wasn't long after that she'd ended up at the punk house in Vancouver.

"You two have been hanging around the Band land down there on the water."

It wasn't a question. It was a point-blank statement. I didn't answer. I just stared at him. We weren't getting anywhere like this.

"Look," I said. "If I knew anything about what happened to her, I would tell you. Aren't you going to look for her? Even if she ran away, what if she's in trouble?"

"That's not how we operate," he said, jotting in his tiny notebook.

Sadie stepped out of the kitchen, almost timid.

"My sister mentioned you'd alerted the Vancouver police."

He nodded. "Sure, but if she's a runaway, there's not much we can do."

"So no one is going to do anything?" I asked. "What if something happens to her?"

But I knew they wouldn't look for her. Even if they found her, they couldn't really force her to come home. She was almost eighteen and she would put up a fight. Sergeant Nygren looked up at me and blinked. He straightened himself, his knuckles popping a little with the shift in weight.

"If you're found down there in the condemned houses, you'll be arrested for trespassing and at the very least fined. You can tell your friends that, too."

Sadie eyed me. This was obviously the first she'd heard about the Sung Spit cabins. I didn't try to hide my contempt for him. I wanted him to leave, but he took his time, straightened up and muttered into his radio. When he finally left, he lingered in the driveway. I wanted to chuck something at him.

Sadie balanced her buttered toast on her teacup and grabbed her bag. She wished me a good day and went out for work. Through the drapes I saw her and the cop talk at the car door.

I woke up the next night after a nightmare about Kendall. She was in the smoke pit outside of the high school and a group of men came up. While one of them tried to get her to come to the back seat of his car, another stood behind her. He reached out, quietly and carefully, and put a cigarette out on her arm. It sizzled. Suddenly it was me in the dream and I could feel the searing burn of the embers. It wasn't the pain that woke me up; it was how I sobbed in the dream, how Kendall sobbed.

I kicked the sheets off and stared at the ceiling while my heart pounded. The sun would be up soon, but not soon enough. No matter how hard I tried I couldn't get my mind off the dream. Eventually, around five thirty, I sat up and pulled some socks on. In the kitchen I forced some cereal down. If I went more than two hours without something, anything, I got dizzy and light-headed. I kept waiting for it to all go away, all of this, but it didn't. It got worse. I'd almost given up praying for my period. There was just the slightest feeling in my gut, like a buzzing and a constant warmth. I couldn't think about it without almost puking.

At quarter to six, the sky lightened as the sun lingered somewhere among the trees. It was going to be a beautiful summer day, the kind when everyone in their right mind was at the beach, a day so endless you could almost think a week had gone by. But I had no interest in it. I was depleted, like a hollow doll. I couldn't imagine what I used to do to pass the time.

I was only five minutes late for my shift at the Village Grocery but when I reached my till my manager was there, waiting.

"Sorry," I said and ushered the next customer over. I could sense my manager looking at my gym shoes. I glanced back and flashed her a smile. She sighed and walked away.

But half an hour into the shift, I started to feel awful. I was light-headed. The only things I could stomach were protein bars from the impulse rack. The wrappers littered the bin beneath my till. I'd pay for them before I left. My body was turning on me and I officially had no allies. Every item that approached on the conveyer belt made me want to chuck.

I picked up a pack of hotdog buns and the queasiness overwhelmed me. I dragged it through the scanner, trying not to dig my nails into it. The next item was a jar of olives. I groaned. I usually loved olives. I tried not to look at the food as I grabbed it and rang it through, and I left it all unpacked at the end of the counter. I forced a smile at the customer, some hippy chick I'd seen on the ferry a few times.

"Twenty-seven fifty," I said and took her cash. Even money made me want to puke with its papery metallic smell. I let the girl shove the groceries into her own cloth bag.

"Hi," I said to the next customer.

"Cassiopeia."

My manager crossed her arms. I turned and tried to suppress an eye roll, unsure if I'd gotten away with it.

"What are you doing?" she asked.

"Working."

"You look like a mentally challenged robot."

I balked. That was rich. I was filing that one away under confidence boosters. I glanced at the next customer's groceries and saw slabs of cellophaned meat and gagged. I turned my back to the awful sight and faced my manager.

"I'm not feeling well today," I said.

This time she rolled her eyes, but didn't try to suppress anything. She flashed a phony smile at the customer and apologized for the wait. Then she leaned in and told me to go home.

"We'll cover your shifts for the rest of the schedule," she said.

"But—"

"You obviously don't want this job. Showing up is not good enough."

She tried to shoo me away, but to my horror, tears began to well. Oh my god, I was about to make a scene in Village Grocery. I hiccupped. My manager's huge, fake smile collapsed when she noticed. I hated Village Grocery but I would go crazy without it. What would I do? Wander the stretch of the island back and forth until someone put me in the nuthouse? I struggled to find the words to explain that I was sorry. I needed the job. I needed the money, too. How would I get to Victoria? I didn't even know how much abortions cost, but I sure as hell didn't have enough in my sock drawer.

"Stop," my manager hissed. "Stop, stop."

She grinned up at the customers and cashiers who were trying not to gawk.

"She's okay!" she beamed. "Just feeling a little sick."

She pushed me to the break room and handed me a tissue.

"Call your mom," she said. "We can talk when you're feeling better."

I sobbed and picked up the phone. It rang and rang, and eventually I just got up and started walking.

At the slope of Arthur's farm, I dragged my feet through the long-grass field with my head down. I pulled the sweaty straps of my backpack from my armpits. A gust of cool ocean air came through the grass behind me and blew my clothes. I knew it was weird to show up, but I had nowhere else to go. Robert was the only friend I had. In the last couple of months, I'd lost Sadie to Pomme, Elliot, and now Kendall.

The red truck wasn't in the driveway. A rooster crowed somewhere behind the house. I stomped up the old steps, sure to make noise. The front door was open. I peered in through the screen.

"Hello?" I called, but no one appeared.

I took a seat on the porch and wondered if it was possible

Robert's lady friend was here. It would make things more awkward, that was for sure. We hardly knew each other but I was beginning to feel comfortable here, slightly entitled to his company.

I listened to the wind rustle the leaves. I closed my eyes and imagined myself an old-time farm wife, back in the day when it might have been perfectly excusable to be pregnant and sixteen. Maybe even admirable if I had working hands and a hearty appetite. There would be ruddy children all over the place; they would basically take care of themselves. If I could just sit here forever and convince myself it was the eighteen-hundreds I might be okay.

But it wasn't okay. I was pregnant. I ran the thought over and over until it made me sick. I'd fucked up. This wasn't make-believe. I opened my eyes and saw the alders ripple in the breeze and the way the sunlight radiated off the ocean beyond the apple trees. No matter how much I wanted it, I couldn't hide here.

I tucked my legs up and sat for a long time. My gut felt like acidic sludge, and every cell in my body was swollen. There was nothing I could do about it and it wouldn't go away. When the sun cast high above the cedars, the truck rumbled down the dusty driveway. A few minutes later, Robert came walking through the yard with mail in his hand. He didn't notice me at first, but when he finally glanced up he looked surprised, then relieved.

"I didn't recognize you." He sat down beside me.

"I was in the neighbourhood," I said dryly. Then added, "It's been a bad day."

"Ah," he said.

"Actually, just a bad year."

"You're too young for that."

I scoffed. If only that were true.

He patted his pockets, pulled out a bag of tobacco and set about rolling it. I eyed him while he did it. It was different from rolling joints.

"A couple of the chickens are getting it pretty bad," he said, pointing toward the coop. "The pecking order. One of them was nearly dead this morning."

"Too many in one run," I said. "They get nervous."

He nodded and I smirked to myself. Maybe I was a farmer in a different life after all.

"So?" Robert asked.

"So." I sighed. "Do you ever drive down to Victoria?"

"Not really. Once in a while."

"What if I paid you?" I asked.

He shifted in his seat. The sun crept into the shade of the porch and burned my bare feet. I tucked them back up under myself.

"I had a bad year once," he said finally. "One bad thing after another, like I was cursed."

"What'd you do?"

He grinned. "Just weathered the storm, I guess."

The rooster cried somewhere in the distance. I bit my fingernails and blinked my tears back. He didn't notice until I started sniffing. I wiped my cheeks.

"Want to talk about it?"

"Yes," I whispered. "But I'm too ashamed."

He leaned forward and placed his hand on my back.

"Not easy at your age," he said.

I shook my head.

"My boy's in Thunder Bay. We only talk once or twice a month."

"You just have a son?"

I waited for him to say something like, as far I know, but he didn't.

"Did you come here a lot when you were younger?"

He nodded and pulled on his cigarette.

"It was my favourite hideout."

I felt the lump in my throat. "I don't know my dad."

He stared at me. "Must be tough."

"Not really," I said, but I couldn't look at him.

❖

When I left Robert's, I walked without thinking about anything for a long time, over the round beach rocks and eventually onto the damp sand when the coastline changed. By the time I got to the houses, it must have been close to four o'clock.

A fresh sheet of plywood barred the door of Kendall's house, but they hadn't bothered with the windows. I rolled my eyes. Break the window, throw a jacket over the edges and you could be inside in a matter of seconds. I squinted through the glass. So she hadn't been here. I wasn't surprised, just disappointed. I wished someone would just torch the places and get it over with. I cupped my eyes and peered through the glare of the single pane. Maybe she was in there, watching me from the damp, moldy living room.

Some of the others were boarded up, ones we hadn't bothered to spend time in, but they'd left the one with brittle, dry bones. I walked up to the doorway and touched the hollyhocks. The smoky blue paint was weathered, so dry and flaky as the wood siding it coated. I picked some off and lingered just outside.

When I was a kid, even a few years ago, I would have been enthralled with this house. I would have swept the thin glass from the drafty floorboards and hiked in linens from Sadie's closet without asking: curtains, a tablecloth for a table I didn't have, and a blanket for the floor to make it seem cozier. For hours I'd busy myself, doing what? I couldn't imagine anymore. Most of all, I'd have convinced myself that I could live here. I'd bring a cooler with some food and maybe a battery-operated radio. Then I would beg Sadie to let me sleep there just one night, and after that I would convince myself that she would be impressed with my independence and let me stay for another night, then another. Then it wouldn't make sense to come home most of the time. It would rain some nights, but I could rig a tarp up on the shingles. In the fall, though, it would get cold and damp. Even as a kid I would have known that. Then what? How could I have gone home again to sleep in my soft bed and, worse, gone back to school for the year after all the solitude?

I sighed. It seemed that I was in a similar position now, except that I wasn't enjoying myself and no one was impressed with me. When I went back to school in the fall, everyone would hear about how I'd been knocked up. Elliot's girlfriend was probably spreading it around town right now. It would be humiliating—I'd probably end up in Alternative because of shame alone. Maybe I'd be expected to fill Kendall's shoes.

I couldn't imagine going back to even a week ago, sitting beside Kendall in the movie theatre that night. Going to a movie with Kendall was more entertaining than watching the movie. She had a knack for humiliating both herself and the people around her at the same time. She had a loud, fake laugh that rang out into the theatre as other people chuckled at stupid jokes onscreen. I think it made most people self-conscious—it had that effect on me, anyway. But I got to laugh with her, and they didn't.

I missed her so hard in that moment, standing in our abandoned village with police tape and plywood all over the place. I couldn't cry or rationalize why she wasn't there. Missing her was a dull ache beneath the ribs, unbearably physical.

When I arrived home that night Sadie and Pomme were cooking pasta. A paper bag of morels sat on the table from their day of mushroom picking. I was ravenous. I sat down and tried to wait patiently for the meal while Sadie danced around the kitchen with her wooden spoon. Patsy Cline was on the stereo and the stovetop steamed and simmered while the sun set behind the cedars. It was almost a nice night despite everything.

Sadie hummed and danced around, her blond feathery hair down her back, and I caught myself wishing she would hug me. I couldn't remember the last time I'd hugged anyone other than grappling Kendall into a one-sided squeeze. I tried to remember what it was like being touched by Elliot, but it was a different lifetime. I hadn't even seen him since that night on the ferry, but every time the phone rang, I half-expected him.

Pomme sliced mushrooms with an intense precision. She hadn't looked up since I came in. Ulla lay under the table and licked her wound. I tried to flick her nose away but she growled. Sadie glanced at Pomme but no one said anything, just poor Patsy walkin' after midnight as pasta water bubbled.

"Cassiopeia, you can set the table," said Sadie.

I got up and put the knives and forks around the table. There was a candle in the centre and a joint. I wondered if they'd let me join them in a pre-dinner smoke, but then Sadie placed the pasta on the table and they sat down. A bottle of red wine sat on the table but Pomme only placed two glasses down and I pretended not to notice.

"Santé," said Sadie with her glass in the air.

"Cheers," said Pomme and her eyes flicked over my heap of pasta.

I nodded and thanked them with spaghetti hanging out of my mouth. I couldn't shovel the food in fast enough. Pomme sighed, put down her fork and stared at Sadie. From the corner of my eye I thought I saw my mother give the smallest shrug.

"What?" I said.

"Nothing," said Sadie.

I rolled my eyes.

"We weren't expecting you for dinner," said Pomme.

"I thought you were at work, that's all," said Sadie. She hated conflict, especially at the dinner table.

"I got sent home early," I said. "My boss called me a retarded robot."

"Cassiopeia."

I shrugged. "That's what she said."

I inhaled my pasta, then eyed Pomme and Sadie's meal. I picked up a lighter and lit the beeswax candle.

"Fancy," I said.

"It's our anniversary," said Pomme.

"Wow."

"Hard to believe," Sadie said. She whisked the hair from my face and tried to smile.

I picked up my plate and helped myself to more at the stove. I ate most of it standing up with my back to them.

"Oh," said Sadie suddenly. "I forgot to tell you. Pomme is taking me to Stuart Island tomorrow."

"Can I come?" I asked.

"Oh, sweetheart—"

"I'm kidding." I sat back down. "Relax."

"We might be gone for a while," she said. "Two weeks maybe."

"Oh."

I looked down at my plate and ran my finger over the tomato sauce. It wasn't the first time Sadie had left me alone. Usually I was happy to have the place to myself, but after a few days it always became lonely.

"I bought lots of groceries and pumped up the bike in the shed."

"Okay," I said, but I couldn't look at her.

I felt tears rising and pinched the insides of my thighs hard to stop myself. No one said anything for a while and I felt the anger bubbling up. I shoved some bread into my mouth.

"Where's my dad?" I asked.

Sadie's face hardened.

"What's his name?"

Sadie tried to compose herself. "I don't know."

"But you must have some idea," I challenged.

She didn't say anything and my nerves kicked up a notch.

"Do you think that's fair?" I asked. "I'm stuck in this shithole with no other family, nowhere else to go and it's supposed to be fine that you were a little slutty—"

"Stop!"

Ulla jumped up and barked.

"Do something about your dog!" I yelled at Pomme.

"I'm sorry, Cassiopeia." Sadie struggled to keep her face relaxed. "I'm sorry. What else can I say? That I shouldn't have had you just because I wasn't sure who your father was? Is that what you want to hear?"

"Yes," I said, feeling pathetic. I was brimming with self-pity. It welled up: pity for my mother, for Kendall and Trish, and then, with a thought that shook me, for the cells frantically multiplying themselves into existence inside of me. That baby was the most pitiful of all of us, at the end of a chain of complete fuck-ups and with no say in it. For a moment, I felt the faintest glimmer of camaraderie for it, and at the same time hatred for myself. In some way, I'd become Sadie. What would she say if she knew? Would she try to convince me to have the baby? But nothing could make me and I knew it was better off this way.

That night I dug through my wastebasket and found papers from my science binder that year. One week someone's mom, a nurse, taught us sex ed. I didn't pay much attention. She showed us how to put a condom on a banana and explained archaic birth control methods. I was already sleeping with Elliot and I smirked in the back row along with half the class. The irony didn't escape me now.

The nurse handed out scraps of paper for questions and told us not to be embarrassed, she would try to answer everything. Only two people wrote legitimate questions, like *can a dude pee when he has a boner?* And, *what's a G-spot?* At the end of the session, she handed out pamphlets. Most were about birth control and clinics, but I dug through them trying to find the one I'd completely dismissed the first time. Pregnancy Options.

I skimmed through the FAQs. My hands shook as I read through abortion methods and timelines. I didn't even really know what it all meant. All I knew was I had to make an appointment. The contact number glared at me from the top of the pamphlet. I clasped the phone between my hands but couldn't dial. I would do it tomorrow, I promised myself. Once Sadie and Pomme left. But the thought of tomorrow made my stomach flip. It wouldn't be easier; it would just get harder and harder.

I gripped the phone and dialed quickly. I didn't know what else to do. The woman answered before I could hang up.

"Hi," I squeaked. "Is Elliot there?"

I tore a nail with my teeth so fast my finger bled. He was the last person I wanted to face, but I didn't have a choice.

"He's away," said his mother. "He's at his cousin's in the Okanagan for a few weeks. Is this Zoe? I thought he told you."

I bit my lip and rolled my eyes to the ceiling. Zoe.

"No," I managed. "No."

So it was official. I was abandoned. The self-pity welled up again but this time terror buzzed along with it. I needed to move, to leave, something. I was strung up, suspended, alone and left to wait.

Beside me, the phone rang.

"Cassie."

The line crackled. My stomach clenched. I stood up and pressed my palm on the door to make sure it was shut tight.

"Where are you?" I asked.

"I'm fine," she said. The phone fuzzed out again and I gripped the handset.

"Meet me somewhere."

"I'm not coming back," she said. She sounded distracted. "I can't talk. I just wanted to say hi. I met some people on the Greyhound and we're going to ride the rails across the country."

"I want to come," I said.

If I started out now, made the last ferry, and barrelled out into

the night I might find her somehow. I stood up and grabbed a bag
from the closet.

"Kendall."

But she was already leaving. No, she was long gone. She was
turning back to her skid friends and forgetting about us. The line
crackled. Traffic roared in the background.

"I'll call you later," she said.

But I didn't believe her. She wouldn't think about us, I knew
she wouldn't. She'd been waiting to leave us all her life. Suddenly, it
was amazing that she'd lasted this long. She would get high and stay
high forever; that's what she wanted. She would be forever moving
on after a lifetime of staying in this one shitty town, on this one
tiny island, with her pathetic family. She knew you blazed your own
way. If you were stuck, you torched your confinements. She'd set
the place ablaze and she'd left me in my half-dumb state to figure
out how to escape. I dropped on the bed, too angry to cry. She had
known the truth long before me: even if she'd brought me with her,
I could never have kept up.

# SUNG SPIT—PART TWO

I OPEN MY EYES to the rattle of grocery carts and the *tink, tink* of glass bottles. The homeless men who squat in the yard next door are sorting their morning haul outside the window of my basement suite. Their conversation is so loud it's like they're hiding under my bed, or in the walls.

The wily cat from upstairs appears at the panes wanting in. Romany adopted it a few months ago. She doesn't believe in getting animals fixed, so he's always aggressive, clambering, eager to cling to an arm like a hammock and gnaw a knuckle. I don't let him in. Romany's about to give birth, a homebirth, upstairs, so she must have cast him out. I strain to decipher the noises upstairs like every time I've been home for the last few days. Is it breakfast, or agony? A bath running, or the midwife? I'm in awe of the girth of her, Romany, my thirty-something-year-old landlady, but also afraid of her. I listen to the sounds so that I can make myself scarce when the time comes.

I clutch the corners of my childhood quilt, the only remnant I have from my mother's home, and pull it over my face. My breath overtakes the rest of the house's sounds. So many people live here— my two roommates, the cat, Romany, her partner, Greg, the friend they rent a room to in their quarters, and Romany's nine-year-old son on alternating weeks. The homeless men next door. One of them, Clive, is the neighbour lady's ex. She lives there with their teenage sons and lets Clive and his buddy hang out. I like that. It's not conventional, and I see it's hard in her strained face behind the curtains and how she avoids the backyard. But it strikes me as a real feat of human nature.

I stay under the blankets until it's unbearably stuffy. My breath labours. Rushing out, pulling in. It sounds like the ocean. Not that the ocean is something to be nostalgic for, just a twenty-minute bike ride from the house. But still. It's something, to be overcome with the tides of oneself. I push the quilt off in a rush of cool air. My hair is greasy. I hear the taps blast somewhere in the house: my roommate snagging the shower first. There's always something to wait for in this house.

Clive and John rattle their way to the back of the property, under the cherry tree by the lawn chairs where they hang out with the slew of teenage boys that congregate. I hadn't seen Clive and John around for a while, was wondering where they'd gone. Sometimes I see them downtown. They don't recognize me when I walk past. I'm just like every other twenty-two-year-old in this city, walking her bike, wearing semi-ironic thrift store clothes part out of style and part out of necessity. Once a couple of old-timers called to me from their alcove. They said, "Hey sister!" and I got a kick out of that. I liked being their sister for a few seconds before I crossed the road.

The phone rings. I hear my roommate whip open the bathroom door and make a dive for it. I ignore her knock at the door and hear her exclaim something about a birthday. Right, it's my birthday. Self-pity wells up. Twenty-three. There's something tragic about turning twenty-three. Twenty-two is my favourite number, it always has been, and now it's gone forever. I sigh and pull the quilt back over my head.

When I'm sure everyone has left the house for the day I venture out. The suite is patched together with old hardwood and slabs of tile. The tile is always cold, even in the summer. Consequently, I'm always cold, down into the very bottom layers of my body. I take a scalding shower. I give myself a whisk of makeup. I comb the tangle of my hair then attempt to cut my fringe with dull scissors. Last time I did it too short. Every time I cut it too short.

On the kitchen table there's an emphatic note from Mary, roommate number one. It says Sadie called to wish me a happy birthday, then in brackets, "Who is Sadie? It's your birthday?!" The space between my ribs, just below my diaphragm, flutters. I haven't heard from Sadie for months, maybe six, and even then only one of those obligatory mother–daughter check-ins. I haven't been home in two years, since Auntie Trish sold the family cabin and we all had one sullen and awkward attempt at celebrating the old place. Some days, maybe on those days when the barometer drops and the clouds suddenly settle in thick and low, I get a yearning to be home, to smell it, to crawl onto the couch, to be hugged. But that passes.

I go to make some toast but the bread is moldy. I boil some water for tea. A mouse appears beside me. I bend down. It doesn't know to be afraid of me. I stand up then stomp on the floor, just beside it, and it scampers away. Sometimes we let Wily Cat in, but mostly we just accept them. Once in a while a compost rat tries to shack up but that is not tolerated, oh no.

I go out and sit under the overhang of the house that acts as a type of patio and sip my tea. Clive and John are busy in the corner of their lot, sorting, bickering. Crows dance in the big oak tree. I tried to make a garden under there even though the soil is dusty and bland. I have some bok choy and cilantro in there that survived the winter. Sadie would not be impressed if she could see this. Once I caught my roommate trying to water it with some flat soda and I yelled at her. I didn't want to waste it, she said. What's the big deal?

I didn't know what the big deal was, exactly, but it seemed wrong. It just seemed wrong.

❖

I get on my bike. Sometimes I work on Thursdays if it's busy. Usually they call if I'm needed, but I swing by anyway. I need the money. It's a restaurant downtown and I'm a barista, bartender kind of thing. Kind of a hip place, I guess. There's always a lineup for breakfast on weekends. The owner goes through phases of hiring the same sorts of people. I got hired in the septum-ring, C-name wave. I guess I walked in at the right moment. She seems a little sick of us now: Cassiopeia, Carla, Cassandra and Celine. She seems to have moved onto boys, particularly grubby ones. One of the cooks in the kitchen is a street kid, and the dishwasher is homeless. I've seen him sitting outside the grocery store with his backpack.

I stroll in and Francis, one of the servers, grins at me.

"Here for lunch?" he asks.

"Do I have to pay?"

He shrugs and tells me Melanie, the owner, is at the bar. I roll my eyes then straighten up. I find her at the espresso machine with a slick, androgynous-looking barista-in-training.

"Oh," says Melanie when she sees me.

"Oh," I say. I get it.

Francis comes over and digs into the till. He doesn't seem to notice the questionable sight behind him. He passes me my cheque and asks if I'm going to the show at Lucky Bar tonight. I ignore him, my fingers curling the edges of my cheque over and over.

"I'll start drinking espresso," I say to Melanie. It's been a point of contention.

"You can keep your Friday shift," she says. "But the weekends. We need someone with a little more flair."

"Flair?" I say. "Shit."

But she's already turned her back. Her hand is on the barista's hand as she shows this person how to tamp just so. I frown. I look down at my cheque. Sixty lousy bucks because it was slow and they sent me home last week. I grit my teeth and force myself to leave before I say something I ought not to.

Outside, it's a cool spring day. I hadn't noticed the day before now. It's the type of spring day that I find terribly depressing. People are wearing shorts, even though they shouldn't be. There are birds. The cherry trees all up and down the street are budding. These sorts of days always strike me as dishonest. Everything is extroverted all of a sudden. I want to know what was so bad about the winter. I want to know why we should all be so happy that the flowers are out. I don't understand what's so great about the flowers. There's no soul to spring; everything is thin and bland and weak.

I leave my bike and cross the road. Down one of the cobblestone streets, I stop at an intercom and press the button. A muffled voice greets me and buzzes me up. The carpeted stairs are narrow and dank. Girls with yoga mats brush by me, elated and released and thinking about what to eat. I pass the yoga studio. It smells like sweat and incense. I used to go there, when I had more money. When I ran out of money I painted one of their bathrooms for free classes, but I used those up so now I'm tense and knotted. Also, I can't remember what it was like to have the motivation to lie down on the floor with thirty other human beings for an hour and a half.

I push the door to the loft. The loft is a shared workspace and also a mecca of all things cool and possible. Everywhere people stand over graphics on computers, print posters, write, play Guitar Hero and drink locally crafted beer while they *discuss*. What, I'm never sure, but they do it with vigour.

"There she is," says Vince.

I open my shoulder bag and pull out the pages I folded into a library book last week. Two reviews of concerts, and one article about a girl in town who makes gourmet ice cream, then bicycles it to your dinner parties.

"They're a little crumpled," I say. "My printer broke."

Vince grins and leafs through them. He nods and grins.

"I might be able to pay you for these," he says. "We might have some new advertisers in the next issue."

I perk up.

"Not much," he says. "But something."

"Great," I say. "Great."

I stand awkwardly for a moment, watching everyone exist so easily. They've all found something. They all came here and carved out a place for themselves. The room is buzzing. The walls are brick and the ceilings are high. A pigeon flies by one of the bay windows; we're high up enough to look down into the streets, off into the distance. Vince clears his throat. I smile weakly.

"I guess I'll see you later," I say.

He nods. He asks if I'm going to the Lucky Bar show, too.

"No," I say. "I don't know. How much is it?"

But that's the wrong question.

"It's my birthday," I say quickly, trying to make amends.

Vince beams and asks how old I am. When I tell him he grips his heart and shakes his head. Apparently I'm young. I don't feel young. He hands me a good-looking bottle of beer from the cooler and wishes me a good day.

"Thanks," I say. It drips on my shoes. I realize I haven't even had breakfast yet. I slip the bottle into my bag and wave. Then I am out, down, into the dark hallway again.

I walk around downtown for a while. I go down to the harbour against my better judgment and get caught in a current of tourists. They walk so slow with their plastic bags and fat shoes. I grumble, dodging them, trying to get up or down a block, away, away. I wish I had someone to call.

I end up in Chinatown. I go into the narrow café with the

coffee bean loft and the row of expertly creative people, alone, hunched over on this Thursday morning. I order a day-old muffin and a cup of coffee.

As the barista hands me my change I ask if they're hiring anyone. He grabs a bar cloth and dusts the register. He accidentally hits some buttons and it lets out a long, constant beep. I know him from somewhere, around. Once I shared a flask with him in line for the club while his girlfriend with the turquoise chest tattoo whined about her heels. He squints at me.

"Not really," he says.

"Well, if you change your mind," I say. I don't want to work here anyway. I like coming here too much.

I go and sit on the curb beside a motorcycle even though there are empty tables on the sidewalk. I like the height of a curb, how my legs drape. I unwrap my muffin and crumbs catch in my bra. I pull out a notebook and write a list of things I need to do.

Number one: Get a new job. Beneath it I scribble: One where I can be left alone to do repetitive, antisocial but still sort of cool things. I think for a while. I don't know what else I need to do, but the constant dissatisfaction buzzing in the back of my head suggests a lot. I pull out a compact mirror and draw a self-portrait. The view is small, so I piece together my eyes and nose and mouth separately, disjointed. I draw the hair and chin from memory. For some reason looking at my chin is too personal, and it's impossible to look at my hair in this mirror. I look down. The drawing is so sad I'm almost embarrassed. I wish I had a cigarette. I don't really like smoking but I enjoy sitting on a curb with a cigarette and a cup of coffee.

I feel a ghost behind me. I turn around and it's my boyfriend, Nick.

"I was in there," he says. "You didn't see me."

"Too hunched," I say.

"You?"

"No, you," I say, straightening up.

He's been on leave from his PhD in philosophy for the last two years. It must be a real stumper. Once I made the mistake of teasing him about it. Turns out it's a touchy subject. He's five years older than me; I guess it's one of those things I won't understand until I'm too old to take a failed project casually. I annoy him, I think, because I'm young and wasting my youth. I'm not excelling in anything, but more than that, I'm not fucking up either. I never get atrociously drunk or high, but I also haven't applied for law school. It seems there's no middle ground with youth. You're supposed to be making the most of it by either getting somewhere or else destroying yourself one hilarious night at a time and I can't seem to do either with much gusto.

Nick looks over my shoulder, at my notebook. I scowl. He grins. I try to frown more severely and slowly close the book.

"It doesn't look like you," he says.

"Thanks," I say, not sure if I'm being sarcastic or not.

He takes my hand and holds it while sort of looking off into the parking lot. I watch him from the corner of my eye. He's not a hand-holder usually. It's about Montreal, I bet. He told me last week that he wants to go back to finish the degree in September and he was hoping I'd come with him. He thought it would be good for me. No pressure.

A car pulls up and waits to parallel park. We get up. The barista comes out, stoops to collect my dishes. He has a long, clean apron on.

"Well," says Nick.

I give him a hug. I've basically taken the Montreal announcement as an indication that we're almost through with each other. I can't tell if he feels the same way. I ask him if he wants to hang out later. It might be nice to have company.

"Depends on how much I get done," he says.

I feel the irrational hurt of someone with a secret birthday. Shouldn't he be more enthusiastic? Isn't that what boyfriends are for? Birthdays? I almost tell him—surely he would be enthusiastic if he knew—but then I don't. I'm just not good at them, boyfriends or birthdays.

◈

I wander up to the industrial part of town. There is no one in this area, except for garage doors and one high-end furniture boutique with many lamps. I like this, being alone on a street, though it's hard, too. Eventually I hit a church with enormous stained glass and turn back toward the people. I stop into the grocery store and wander back to the deli where my friend Cory works. I used to work here, too. Maybe I should ask for my old job back. Maybe I'm actually not too good for a deli.

Once she convinced me to eat a hash granola bar with her during the evening shift. We crouched behind the sandwich bar and ate it. Then I realized she was going home in an hour and I would be left alone for another six. She laughed evilly and I felt myself coming up hard as I handed a pound of sliced turkey breast to a woman with a sun hat, thinking, no, no, shit. For the rest of the night, I washed dishes in the corner and ignored customers.

I find her hanging up her apron by the back door. She has the short morning shift. She makes elaborate meals for rich urban singles who don't feel like cooking. She tackles this job with an intensity, bringing recipes from home, focusing on presentation. She's moved from mac and cheese to portabella mushroom steaks and mashed potatoes with delightful garnishes. She grins when she sees me and ushers us out the back door. Everything she does has an air of rebellion and conspiracy. She wears makeup and clean clothes, and gets to work on time, but no matter what she does you can always tell who she really is. She has an anarchistic heart that pulses out for anyone to see.

We walk away from downtown, back toward our houses. She rents a room in a tall character house on the outskirts of the industrial area and lower Fernwood. It's a strange corridor for drug addicts and bottle collectors. The houses are dilapidated and brittle one block, and painted and cheerful the next.

As we walk she tells me about a photography class she's taking. She's getting into film and do I know anyone who has access to a darkroom? I shrug. She reminds me of Kendall. Sometimes I want to ask her if she's ever sucked cock for cigarettes, but I don't want to embarrass her. I think she's at a place in her life where it would embarrass her. But I want to know because knowing would quench something in me. I would feel at ease if I had a surefire Kendall figure in my life. I could project all hope onto Cory, convince myself that Kendall has grown into a person just like Cory. Anarchistic, punk-ass, but seriously trying to be passionate about the shit she's stuck with. Inspired; or at least intelligent enough to know she has to act inspired. I presume Cory is depressed. In fact, I've seen her pill bottles in the cabinet. But at least she's functioning. Sometimes that's the best you can hope for in a young woman.

We wander up through the quaint streets of Fernwood and stop in the community garden. Cory wants to smoke pot. I never much feel like smoking pot anymore, but I usually end up doing it. We find a bench and sit down. I don't tell her it's my birthday. She might try to take it too far. I'm not looking for a good time, I realize. I don't know what I'm looking for, but I think it involves heading home for the afternoon and sulking.

Cory rolls a joint. She never lets me roll. I think she assumes I can't do it properly. Sometimes I look at her and miss Kendall intensely. Sometimes I want to reach over and kiss her on her mouth, but I don't know why. Maybe to prove to myself that she's not Kendall. She always wears lipstick and she has yellow teeth.

"Are you still seeing that guy?" Cory licks the rollie.

"Meh," I say, but there's a lump in my throat.

The birds sound less offensive in this garden. Like they belong here, and their songs are muffled by the spring flowers, which also aren't so bad in this landscape. I pull my feet up on the bench and relax. There has been a string of bad and mundane days for as long as I can remember, and this day is no different but this moment. I crave moments like this, when I can just exist. But as soon as I recognize it, it's gone. Or the sun shifts just so. Or too many cars go by and everything gets flipped.

Cory gets bored and starts pointing at the different plants around us. It's our game and a constant source of amusement for her. I know the name of almost every plant everywhere.

"Calendula," I say blandly.

She points.

"Lavender. Russian sage. Fennel."

She shakes her head in disbelief.

"Black-eyed Susan. Lemon balm. Redcurrant." I squint. "No, gooseberry."

"God," she says. Her eyes are pink. "You're such a fucking hippy."

We're running out of plants. She searches the perimeter and points.

"That's a potato." I glance at her. Sometimes I just make it up if I don't know.

"I saw him the other night," says Cory, eyeing me.

"Where?" I get a sick feeling. Sometimes I'm convinced everyone will leave me. "What was he doing?"

"At the grocery store," she says. "Relax."

"He's moving to Montreal," I say, realizing he *is* possibly going to leave me. I wave the smoke away from my face even as I grip the joint and take a hit. A fake hit. A quick one. I don't feel like being alone and stoned on my birthday, but Cory wouldn't understand. "He wants me to come with him."

"No," says Cory, her eyes gleaming.

I glance at her. If it were possible, if it would make her happy to move to Montreal with a man, I would gladly forfeit the opportunity to her. She would do it just for the story, for the experience, even if she knew it would make her miserable. She asks if I'm going.

"I haven't really thought about it," I say.

It's not true though. I think about it all the time, the essence of a faraway city seeping into my thoughts constantly, taunting me, thrilling me. I think about going away with this guy and being sad in a foreign city. Something about it appeals to me. I imagine myself there like I'm writing me into a story. A character in a window. It's awfully self-indulgent.

Cory is talking about Montreal. I didn't know she'd been. She's talking about *super sexe*, and an intaglio school there. She's talking about the bakeries, too. A secret rooftop greenhouse run by Concordia students. I listen. Everyone has a different Montreal, but most of them circle the same enigmatic essence.

"Meh," I say again. I'm scared of Montreal.

She shoots me a sour look.

"If it were me—" she says.

"You could," I say. What's stopping anyone?

"This town is dead."

I agree with her, but it doesn't seem an excuse to leave. If it's dead you do something about it. Otherwise you accept that it's probably you who's dead, contributing to a whole city of likewise people. The thought of going somewhere where all the fun is laid out for you seems backwards somehow. It seems cheap.

"I just don't think you should take a guy like that for granted," she says.

I snort and she seems genuinely pissed off at me. Maybe she knows something I don't, being a whole three or four years older. I bend down and rip at a plant and shove it in my mouth.

"Parsley," I say, hoping to lighten the mood. As I chew, I realize I might have misidentified. I don't want her to doubt my botanical talent, though, so I swallow it.

"Look," says Cory, shifting on the bench to face me. She's revving up. "What are you doing here? I mean, seriously. You're miserable."

"Not the town's fault." I'm not trying to stand up for our city, just to explain that there's something fundamentally off that's not going to go away just because I pack up my shit and move.

"You need to be more passionate about something," she says. Her face is red. I've never seen her so confrontational. She's usually more of a smooth talker.

"Good god," I say. She sounds like someone else's mother. I remind her she makes sandwiches for a living and she slaps her thigh so loud I flinch. She bites her lip, just beside the lip ring she has to remove for work.

"Go," she says.

"But why?"

Cory groans, fed up with me.

"No, seriously," I say. "What's so great about going? It's not going to be any different just because I'm somewhere else."

"How do you know?"

I try another tactic. "I don't know how to live properly."

Cory flicks her lighter and laughs. My face is blazing. It's true, though. My life hasn't started yet. Montreal isn't going to kick-start it. I just know it. Cory is quiet for a while; then she shakes her head.

"That's the biggest load of bullshit I've ever heard."

I glare at the gardens, out past the lavender. Maybe it sounds like bullshit, but suddenly I know it's true. I've been waiting for something. I've been alternating between frantically trying to get there and lying back, almost helplessly. I look at Cory. Her face is more relaxed now. She's thinking of something else. Maybe *super sexe*. I know she's going to crack some jokes, her way of apologizing for getting in my face. I'll shrug and say something like, yeah, well, whatever.

When we do get up to go our separate ways, we give each other a tight hug. I don't know when I'll see her again. We never make plans, just find each other when the time is right. I don't know what it will take for me to stop in at the grocery store again, though I'm not mad at her. I just don't need her right now. She's a force travelling in the opposite direction.

She heads toward her place, and I turn in through the gardens to head home. I feel very alone. I think of Nick, what it will feel like if he leaves in a couple of months and I don't go with him. A small twinge of sadness catches me. Mostly I think I'll miss his room. His narrow bed, the curtains drawn tight to the street lamps, the tattoos on his arms that I circle over and over again. I think about my friends at the restaurant who I won't see much anymore. I need a new job. I'll make new friends; I'll run into the old ones. But I'll miss just seeing them first thing in the morning, watching them haughty and stressed when we get slammed. Hungover and trying their best. That's the kind of thing that makes a family, really. But these ones come apart easily.

Then I think of Sadie calling me on my birthday. Last year she forgot, or at least she didn't call. What did it take this year? I picture the wall where the calendar has hung since the beginning of time. I imagine my name with a heart on today's square. I imagine her rifling through scrap paper or her address book where my name surely has many crossed-out numbers from all the times I've moved from one place to another. How she picks up the phone, risks the last number she has for me. I imagine her hands on the receiver. The smell of her clothes. It makes me dead tired and sad.

I'm halfway home when I realize I forgot my bike downtown. It'll be gone by sunset, or else stripped to a carcass, if I don't go back for it. My legs are tired and my shoes are tight. All I want is to be home, to crawl back into bed or let Wily Cat in to trash my room. But that bike is almost all I've got, so I go back for it.

Heading home, I make long loops through the neighbourhood. It's late afternoon somehow. It's my favourite time of day. The sun hits

Fernwood so full and golden where everywhere else is in shadow, or hues of pink and orange. The sky is clear. My hands are a little cold on the metal handlebars but my hands are always a little cold. I coast down the quaint, funky streets and my heart breaks and blooms at the same time. I love these houses. Character houses, they call them, except these ones actually have character, painted vibrant blues or golden yellows. Gardens overcome lawns, patches between sidewalk and road. I let a hill take me, close to home now. There's an open window and someone plays the piano.

When I get home, there's some commotion in the upper house but I don't see anyone. I don't hear any newborn's strange and creature cry. I hop off my bike and walk it down the driveway, lean it against the staircase. Clive and John are gone but their shopping cart is still here. I dig for the keys in my bag then notice Wily Cat in the yard. He's batting at something with such boredom I almost laugh. I wander over, then gasp. A hideous rat is half-mauled on the grass, its teeth slats of yellow, its eyes rolling.

"Bad," I scold the cat. He crouches there and bats the thing into submission every time it tries to get away. It's so ugly. I hate the rat. Yet I'm filled with pity for it.

I try to walk away. I wander into the kitchen and drop my bag. No one has been here since me. I pick up the half-cup of cold tea from the counter and drink it. It's been steeping for hours and it's bitter. The ceilings are low in our little suite and I feel someone walking above me. I hear some chatter.

Through the open door I see Wily crouched, batting. I cringe. I walk back out and realize the rat has tried to make a slow and pathetic getaway, and is headed toward our front door. I drop my tea on the outdoor bench and slam the door.

"Finish it off," I tell the cat. I tell him he's being cruel. But it's not about that anymore. It's about a half-dead rat in the house. I think of a rat helping itself to our food. I think of the kilo of rice I just lost to moth maggots spinning a web in the dark folds of grain.

I can't afford another loss like that. Beside, who knows where that rat might end up.

"Wily Cat," I say again, stern, as the rat drags itself on the grass. The cat seems to understand, strolls over and bats the thing with a tad more vigour. But not enough.

"Kill it," I hiss at him, then glance up and realize the neighbour's eight-year-old is standing on her porch watching me. I give a little wave. I clasp my forehead and indulge myself, as I know what I have to do next, in the thought that this is the worst birthday ever. I go to the shed and find a shovel.

When it's done, I'm exhausted and shaking. My arms are not accustomed to killing. They tensed at the moment before impact, resulting in light pity blows just like the cat's. He stepped back in to do some claw-work when I just couldn't, when I felt tears coming up. It was worse that the rat was ugly, and that it was destined to die. That anyone at all would understand the impulse to kill it. When I was sure it was dead, I flicked the rat onto the shovel and buried it in the loose rocky soil behind the shed.

Inside, I sit on the couch. Wily Cat saunters in and collapses on the hardwood beside me. He licks his paws, but my hands are shaking. I need to wash them, but can't make myself get up. It's my birthday, heading into the evening, but the day seems like it might never end.

I catch a glimpse of someone through the kitchen window, then hear something in the backyard. Romany. Shuffling around the back grass with her hands gripping her enormous belly. I know without knowing: it's happening. She stops for a long moment and hangs her head. I see fear in her face when she straightens back up. She catches my eye and holds up a hand in greeting. I wave back, meekly. I feel the irrational guilt of someone not in labour. I feel, suddenly, like bolting.

The midwife joins her in the yard. They converse, Romany's hands flapping, then pausing, tensing, gripping. I imagine them spreading blankets right there, right beside my garden, Romany crouching. It's ridiculous, I know it is, but I'm afraid. I don't know what I'm afraid of. I'm afraid of the moment it becomes real, the moment that creature slips out and everyone is joyful, relieved. I'm afraid of only terror in that moment, when everyone else is gleaming. I get up and pace the living room. Then, behind Romany, poor, terrifying Romany, I see a crow. It's dragging something out behind the shed. It's dropping the soft, heavy body of the rat into my garden.

I slam the car door and shove my bag into the back seat. Nick gets into the driver's seat and we sit for a moment. I adjust my seat back, so I'm almost reclining, and rest my head. The midwife's car is parked in front of us.

"Were you working?" I ask.

He shrugs. He was. I'm that girl, the hysterical one, who things need to be dropped for. I think he likes it, though. He seems content enough to be needed. He fiddles with the gearshift and asks where we're going. He's imagining a drive to the lakes, then Vietnamese, I'm sure. I'm imagining him dropping me off in the middle of nowhere so I can walk home alone.

Down the sidewalk, I see Clive and John trundling with another cart. Nick watches them. I don't think he's met them. We usually sleep at his house. I roll my window down as far as it will go. Clive stops a couple feet from the car and grins. He's got an orange beard and a red face, long fingernails. Something about him makes me think: imitation crab.

"Hi," I say. I point to the house. "The baby's coming."

"Ooh," he says and straightens up. I bet he's seen a lot of babies born in his life, though I couldn't back that up. He just strikes me.

He leans in to the car a bit, hand clasped on the rim of the window frame.

"The shelter's got a lot of food right now," says Clive.

I nod. His face is a few inches from my face. Then he straightens up and comes back gripping two immaculate cauliflowers. He pushes one toward me, drops it on my lap, then pushes the other one through.

"Thanks," I say, staring down at them. "It's my birthday."

They're heavy and dense on my lap. I realize I'm actually quite hungry, and they cheer me up somehow.

"Well," says Clive. John has trundled away, lost interest. "You'll have the same birthday as the baby."

I hadn't thought about that. I hold the cauliflower closer, and watch Clive turn down his ex-wife's driveway. I turn to Nick. Am I the strangest girl he's been with? I place the cauliflower on the back seat next to my bag. I realize I forgot my toothbrush inside. I'm not going back in now. I'm on my way out.

"How much time do you have?" I ask Nick.

"You didn't tell me it was your birthday."

"I'll give you gas money."

"No." He shakes his head.

"Or maybe you could drive me to the bus depot."

"Just, where."

"I think I have to go home," I say.

I got a letter from Kendall once. It must have been four years ago. The summer I left home. She'd mailed it to Sadie's house in a bank envelope, the ones with the filmy plastic window, with no return address. The way Sadie handed it to me, I knew she felt conflicted. She wanted to respect my privacy, but she could guess who it was from and also felt she should confiscate it, hand it over to Trish. I think she was hoping I would do the right thing, give these poor mothers some indication of where she was or what she was doing, but I didn't. I burned it in the backyard after I read it. It was a gesture of great sacrifice because I wanted more than anything to keep it and look at her handwriting over and over again, read and reread her words to create new more hopeful meanings. But I thought Kendall would want me to destroy it. Looking back on it, maybe she had secretly hoped I would leave it lying out somewhere. Maybe she wanted her mother to know, to come looking for her, or to suffer.

The letter read:

~~Cassie~~ Cous! *How are you? I've been travelling. I was just living in a shelter in Toronto. I met a guy and we lived together, then I found out he had a wife and kid in Halifax. What a prick. I got hooked on speed for a while. I got really skinny you wouldn't recognize me. But I'm better now. Love you, Special K*

Special K. A drug the kids at Alternative used to do. A shelter, a guy, drug addiction. But she was better now. I'm better now. I thought about that last line almost every day. I never believed it. How could she be better now? I'd looked up all the shelters in the Toronto area and even tried to call some of them. No one answered, or no one wanted to talk, or sometimes I just couldn't muster the courage.

A couple of years ago, after Trish sold the cabin and we went to help put things in boxes, Trish mentioned she'd heard from Kendall. She'd moved down to Philadelphia. I asked if she had a number for her, and Trish laughed and said, are you kidding? Like it was the stupidest thing I'd ever said. An old tinge of anger came back to me, wondering why she hadn't looked harder, why she wasn't a better mother. But I knew by that point that she had tried. She'd hired someone. They'd found her, tracked her, then lost her. She was too old to be dragged home. She wasn't destroying herself, not in any immediate danger.

And I knew that it was killing her. Trish had aged ten years in just a couple. Her face was puffy and yellow-grey. Her voice had gotten rougher. Sadie said she was drinking. Lucas didn't come around much, either. He'd tried a year of private school then moved to Campbell River and one of his friend's moms let him live with them while he finished high school. He came over on weekends to visit Trish for a while, but then he just stayed away. She wasn't an easy person to be around.

I thought about Philadelphia. It seemed the farthest, most convoluted city. It seemed impossible that it existed. She might as well have been in a dark nook on the edge of the world. What was she doing there? Sometimes I called Trish, but there was nothing to talk about. All I wanted was to ask. But she never knew.

We pull off at a gas station near Parksville. Nick goes in to scrounge some food and I go to the pay phone to call Sadie. I punch the numbers like it's nothing, tap my foot and refuse to think about what I'm going to say until the answering machine comes on. I start to leave a loud, casual message about being on the road with my boyfriend. We thought it might be cool to come over for the night. Sadie picks up. I'm quieter. Is it okay? Yes, of course, come over. I strain to hear the sub-notes in her voice but can't.

We drive. Nick asks me what my mom is like; I haven't told him much. I shrug. He knows I don't go home much. He thinks, maybe, it's an angsty remnant of my adolescence. He thinks we just don't get along.

"She's …" I say. I don't know what to say.

I try to be objective, but every adjective I think of has connotations for me. She's a hippy: she has outlandish values that she imposes on people. She's sweet: she's not a critical enough thinker. She's laid-back: she doesn't take the strain of hardships seriously enough; she's not compassionate in the right places.

I've told Nick about Kendall. I've talked about her so much that we mention her in conversation like she's a mutual friend. I love that about him, that he's adopted her, that she's alive in the space between us. He knows I don't have a dad; he doesn't have one either. He grew up with "a father figure" but he came too late, too politely. It's something we laugh about. Bastards. I told him about how I followed a neighbour around that summer Kendall left, convinced he was my father. We laugh; he's done that, too.

When we get to Campbell River, we pull off the highway and glide right onto the second-to-last ferry. On the car deck, Nick steps out of the car and stretches. I sink further into my seat. He wants to go up and walk around the top deck, feel the wind flap his cheeks.

"It's not that kind of ferry," I say, sitting put.

I have to pee so bad it hurts to move, but I cannot face the passenger deck. I'm not ready to launch into the intimacies of a ferry crossing. Nick strolls around the car deck. I see his silhouette on the bow of the boat. He's probably never been on a ferry like this, I realize. He's from somewhere outside of Toronto. When the ferry prepares to dock, he flops back into the car. He smells like the freshest air, and salt spray.

It's humid and cool as we pull into the driveway, the windows rolled down. My cheeks are hot, and my body is buzzing. The lights are on in the kitchen. The whole house glows in the spring night.

I catch a glimpse of her through the window, behind the lace, and my heart jumps. I feel ill. I regret coming. Nick parks the car. I turn to him, want to explain somehow the dread rising in me, the fear, but he gets it. I can tell by his face. He's patient. He wants to say something reassuring but isn't sure what.

Then Sadie appears on the deck, the shadow of her beside the old claw foot and behind the grapevines. She looks different. A haircut, maybe. Older and younger at the same time. I get out of the car. I reach into the back seat and grab the cauliflowers. They're awkward. I hold one in each hand like they're the secret to keeping me safe.

I walk up and Sadie pulls me in for a hug. I hold the cauliflowers behind her back, and it results in a cold, one-sided hug.

She doesn't seem to notice, or is pretending not to. Gives me a kiss. She pulls away and greets Nick like she knows him. They do their own introductions, I don't have to speak, I stand aside. Sadie smiles warmly. I catch her eye and we both look away. She's trying, and that scares me, that she's trying and not just happy to see me. I'm trying, too. The layers of this evening make me nervous.

We go inside. I run for the bathroom. I pee in the dark. The counters are lower than I remembered. Everything seems too short or too tall. The toilet is too short, the bathtub so tall. I stand in the middle of the room, letting my eyes adjust. Nick and Sadie talk in the kitchen, loudly, enthusiastically. They'll get along fine. I'm not worried about them. I flick water from my hands, then grope for a towel. I will touch as little as possible, I decide. I will remain in my private bubble. I will spend a day here, observe, be reminded of how strange home is, then I won't need to return for another year or so. Even as I tell myself this, I feel the armor more like eggshell, cracking, flaking.

Sadie pours us a glass of wine and finds some old Scotch in the cupboard for Nick. She puts her feet up on a kitchen chair. Soup stock simmers on the stove. We talk like there's nothing much to talk about. The chickens are gone. She gave them to a young couple with a hobby farm in Quathiaski Cove. Pomme is gone, too, I notice, though she's been on the outskirts for a while now. It was getting too hard to look after them, the chickens, what with her work. She speaks more to Nick than me.

When Nick asks her what she does, I get up and rummage through the cupboards. Popcorn, I decide. There's knobby and streaked apples still stored from the fall. I take one of those, too, and wash it. The flesh is soft and mealy. Already being in the kitchen, touching things, remembering where the knives are, the plates, I can feel myself reverted, concerned.

"I'm a doula," Sadie tells Nick. I blast the tap and scrub the apple. "I work mostly with teen mothers up and down the Island."

"Ah," Nick nods.

He doesn't know anything about me, I realize. We're basically strangers, and now he's in my childhood kitchen. I feel sick. Sadie is nodding and talking, rambling. She loves talking about her work. It's replaced something in her, it seems. She's not the same; she is defined by this job. She's become something fierce, like there's not enough time in the day to help all the teenagers become empowered in their pregnancies. Sadie is talking about poverty now, the lack of empowerment in poor communities, and how it doesn't have to start with funding, it has to start with the people. But of course the funding is important.

I chop the apple. The knife is dull and it slips this way and that. Nick asks how she got into this sort of work. She pauses and thinks about it. Careful not to look at me, careful not to appear to even think about me. She's looking back into her motivations and carefully avoiding me. It's an agreement we've come to, somehow, silently, over the years. Something we never talk about.

"I think the day it became *real*, you know, when you just know you've found your calling," she says. Nick nods. "I was doing my training and had been assigned to check in on a woman in a remote community. I was driving out there, and my car broke down on the side of the road. I mean, this was almost in the middle of nowhere. I had no cellphone reception, very few houses along the highway. So I had to flag a car down. I waited for probably an hour before I even saw anyone, and then a car appears."

I've heard this story before somehow. It's a story she's been using to redefine herself since she became a doula the summer after I left. A neat and tidy one. She sits up, her eyes dancing for Nick.

"The car stops and I get in. The back seat is full of groceries, crap, and beside me is a baby, maybe six months. And the mother is driving, her friend is beside her, and they're so young, you know, seventeen, eighteen maybe. I say, oh thanks, you know, my car broke down, and they say no problem, we're going right into town, we live there. And halfway along the drive they crack some cans, like coolers or something. And they just start drinking and laughing like it's no big deal at all, nothing abnormal about driving toward the teen suicide capital of the country while drinking and driving with a baby in the back seat, in the back seat with a hitchhiker. I wanted to get out but didn't want to leave this baby. I wanted to sit with this baby for a while. But I think what really got me was the smell. The whole car smelled like, like, that sweet baby smell and sugary booze. It disturbed me."

"Wow," says Nick.

Sadie laughs and slaps the table. So that was it, she says. Something in her changed that afternoon and she knew she really wanted to help these women realize their potentials, and for her it starts with the pregnancy, it starts with the birth.

I plug the popcorn maker in and it whirls. Nick and Sadie look at me, like they'd forgotten I was there, or like they're expecting me, the link between them, to contribute to the conversation, to the moment. I look away. I look for butter in the fridge but all I find is a tub of vegan crap. I don't want to ask. I look dig deeper and find some coconut oil. Nick's mother had him young, eighteen. I want to change the subject before they latch onto it but can't think of anything to say. I unplug the popcorn maker instead of adding kernels. I don't feel hungry anymore.

I slip away. I go to my room and fumble through the dark for my bedside lamp. It's not there. I find it on the desk. Everything looks sparser, tidier, but I can't tell what's missing. Everything is familiar, but lacking meaning. It's nice; it makes it easier to be here.

The bed sags under me. I think of my bed back in Victoria and it seems so far away. The house of mice, of people living above me, their feet just feet from my head, Wily Cat, the cold, damp floor: it's all depressing. It's my life, and from this distance it doesn't look like much. It seemed fine up close, but from far away it's scattered and struggling. I try to think of things I love there: my bicycle, the way the light hits the top hill in Fernwood, the cafés, the walk through long, winding streets to the ocean. Some of the things I could take with me, some of them I couldn't. Some of the bad things would follow me, and some of them wouldn't. I drape my arms over my face. I hear a toilet flush, the bathroom door open. I think about going to rescue Nick; then there's a soft knock on the door. I sit up. Sadie crosses the room and smiles. I tense. She holds a little package out.

"Happy birthday," she says. "I actually bought it last birthday and never got around to giving it to you."

I open it. It's a necklace with a small clear stone.

"It's white topaz," she says. "Your birthstone. Well, actually it's supposed to be diamond, but you know."

It's the kind of gift only a mother could get away with and it's touching in spite of my resistance.

"Thanks," I say, slipping it on. "It's pretty."

"Well." She shrugs. "I know it's not much."

I want to tell her about the moths in my rice, and the rat this afternoon, about how the cauliflowers are from a food bank. How I'm barely getting by, but how it's exhilarating sometimes. I want to tell her about how Romany is probably giving birth *right now* and about my garden. I want to ask her what she thinks about Montreal.

She makes like she's going to stand up, but then stay. She motions to the kitchen.

"He seems nice."

"Yeah," I say.

"No, really though," she says. Something about her is clearer, more present. I wonder what I look like to her. Can she tell by my face exactly what my life is like? "He seems like he really cares about you."

"We don't know each other very well," I say.

She thinks I'm being stubborn, but I'm not. I haven't told him much about myself. I haven't told him how I was just like his mom, just like Sadie. How I waited and waited to tell anyone until it was too late for a simple procedure. How Sadie thought it was unethical. Unethical. Immoral. That I should finish what I'd started, take responsibility for my mistakes, my layers of mistakes.

It was too late and I should have told someone sooner. I should warn him that I'm selfish and cowardly. How I often wonder if she was right, but I did it anyway and I hated myself for it. Then we lived in this house together for another year, hating each other while I struggled through school, because I was too defeated. I should tell him how we couldn't understand the same things; how Sadie could understand something I couldn't, chose to put her faith in something other than her daughter. I look at her. I want to plead with her. I want her to just make it okay.

She smiles, almost sad, but unwilling to join me in it. She clasps her hands.

"Well." She tries to find the right words. "You're still young. You have your whole life."

I feel the tears rise up.

She says, "It's okay."

She holds me, rocks me and says it's okay. I let her because she has to, because she's my mother.

I wake up too early, unable to get back to sleep. Nick beside me on the double bed, limbs too long, asleep and heavy and draped over me. I get up to go to the bathroom. I stop in the kitchen for water. It's just after six. The sun isn't up, but the sky is lightening. I notice something on the table. An envelope with my name on it propped up against a vase. The return address somewhere in Montana. I flip it over. Sadie's writing on the back, a phone number, the beginnings of a grocery list, as though she realized what she was writing on and stopped. How long ago did it arrive?

My hands tremble. I go back to the room and stand there, staring at Nick. I want to wake him up, but then decide I'd rather be alone. I find his car keys in his pants and get dressed.

There's frost on the car, but not much. I start the engine and let it rumble in the driveway. I expect to see someone on the porch, sleepy, watching me, but no one comes out. The letter on the seat beside me. I drive the island. I'm the only one on the road. At the intersection to the village I slow at the lights and gaze at the plaza. It looks better than it used to, but I can't pinpoint it. The café is just opening; a woman carries a sandwich board out and wipes a table down. I turn before the ferry, not knowing what I'll find. The last time I was here, they'd flattened the houses, pulled pieces out with the delicate precision of machinery claw, one piece at a time in a scheme to appear environmentally sensitive. It could all be homes now. It could be private property.

I park by the old trail, now a wide mud road of tractor wheels There's a billboard nailed to some posts outlining the development plans. An artist's rendition. Twenty-six townhouses. Old trees replaced with perky urban trees. A brick pathway before the beach. I'm not surprised. I know enough by now not to be surprised by the way the world works. But I'm still disappointed.

I walk down. The trees are sparser, but the light comes in nice. In the distance I see development but when I get closer it's smaller than I expected. It's the framework, timber and plywood. The forest around it has been flattened for machines here and there, but it's not so different.

I shake some scaffolding to the second storey and climb before I chicken out. I put the letter in my mouth and don't look down. I heave myself up, my fingernails on the gritty plywood. The ocean is spread before me, flat and pure and metallic with the sun rising. It's cold-looking. I sit and wrap my sweater tight. The envelope. A return address in the left-hand corner: Absarokee, Montana.

I open it. There's a photograph of a woman on a horse. I frown
and unfold the letter. My eyes trail over the writing, scanning, trying to understand, but can't piece anything together. I flip it over,
double-sided, small print. I force myself to slow down, let my eyes
travel to the signature at the bottom. Hers. I grip the paper and start
over. I read. Something about leaving the band in Philadelphia, as
though I should know, as if I knew all this time she was just living
and playing in a band. Then she went to rehab. Pretty much everyone in rehab finds Jesus, but don't worry, she didn't. She thinks she's
going to be okay. Taking it one day at a time, you know. Anyway,
she wants to say sorry for being a shitty cousin. She knows it wasn't
easy on us, her leaving like that. She hopes it all worked out okay.

She met a man in Montana on her way back to Canada. He's
got two kids who visit him on weekends. But how was I? Casual:
what was I up to these days? He owns a ranch, the man, two hundred acres, stretching all the way to the Stillwater Valley. He's older,
maybe I can tell. But he's okay, he's better than okay. And she's
learned to ride. She takes tourists on trail rides. She has a stallion.
She's the only one who can ride him. It's nice being up there in the
sagebrush.

I drop the letter and pick up the photo. I look closely at her
face. How? I ask her. How? Everything is different. Her grin is not
her grin, like she's taught herself how to smile at different things,
smile for different reasons. She's bigger and healthier. I let it flood
me: relief and confusion and frustration. The feeling that we will
never, ever have her; that even if she's good, she will be out there
and never here.

I laugh. I look at her face. Her eyes. The same devious eyes,
but shining for some new thrill now. My eyes wander down, past
her fingers tangled in her horse's mane, gripping, bareback, over her
body. I look at her horse. Of course it's a stallion. I can see the spirit
in him through the photo. He reminds me of her; their eyes. He's
slightly blurred like he's just about to take off. Like he's pausing only

for the briefest second, to indulge someone on the other side of the camera who has waited for a long time to capture him, just for a second, before he rears up—her hands gripping his mane, clenching her thighs—to skitter away.

# ACKNOWLEDGEMENTS

Well, firstly, I'd like to tip my hat to anyone who ever believed me when I insisted that I was a writer, even though I never let you read a word. Especially Doug and Leonie, my parents. Your faith gave me courage, or at least enough delusion when it counted the most. I'd also like to thank all the workshop buddies who waded through my first drafts over the years, and for being good drinking buddies and inspiring writers, too. Jen Neale and Karim "Old Man" Alrawi come to mind. John Gould, Bill Gaston, Andreas Schroeder, Steven Galloway and Annabel Lyon—thanks for encouraging me. I know it's your job, but, thanks.

The biggest acknowledgement of all goes to Alex: fellow writer, personal editor and endlessly supportive husband.

PHOTO JESS LONG

BORN TO BACKPACKING ski bums in the eighties, Janine Alyson Young read every appropriate book in her town's library before age eleven. She attends the MFA program in creative writing at UBC and lives with her husband and son on the Sunshine Coast, where she runs a taco stand with an architect. Her work has appeared in *This Side of West*. *Hideout Hotel* is her debut collection.